# MAGICAL
# SEDUCTION

# MAGICAL SEDUCTION

CATHRYN FOX

MANDY M. ROTH

ANYA BAST

POCKET BOOKS
NEW YORK   LONDON   TORONTO   SYDNEY

Pocket Books
A Division of Simon & Schuster, Inc.
1230 Avenue of the Americas
New York, NY 10020

First Pocket Books trade paperback edition April 2008

POCKET and colophon are registered trademarks of Simon & Schuster, Inc.

For information about special discounts for bulk purchases,
please contact Simon & Schuster Special Sales
at 1-800-456-6798 or business@simonandschuster.com

Manufactured in the United States of America

10 9 8 7 6 5 4 3 2 1

Library of Congress Cataloging-in-Publication Data

Magical Seduction / Cathryn Fox, Mandy M. Roth, Anya Bast.—1st Pocket
Books trade pbk. ed.
     p.   cm.—(Ellora's Cave anthologies)
        1. Erotic stories, American. 2. Occult fiction, American. I. Fox, Cathryn.
Web of desire. II. Roth, Mandy M. Solo tu. III. Bast, Anya. Tempted by two.
PS648.E7T46 2008                                    813'.60803538—dc22

ISBN-13: 978-1-4165-7721-8
ISBN-10:      1-4165-7721-1

# CONTENTS

# WEB OF DESIRE

## CATHRYN FOX

# PROLOGUE

As Ally Shears approached the old abandoned mansion, she felt her stomach knot and her mouth go dry. She hated what she was about to do, but knew she had little choice in the matter. Mentally reciting the banishing spell from her *Book of Charms*, she reached into her jeans, her fingers connecting with the packet of herbs needed to send her cousin to the netherworld.

Dodging a low-hanging branch that fringed the walkway, she made her way down the narrow path leading to the decrepit house on Manor Drive. The soothing scent from a nearby lilac reached her nostrils but did little to ease her ragged nerves. With light footsteps, she crept up the stairs in search of Selina. Even though Ally hated the task before her, she knew it was best for the townsfolk. Banishing her cousin to the netherworld was a much better alternative than what the angry women of the town would likely do to Selina for using witchcraft on their beloved men.

If her cousin couldn't abide by the council's rules and use her witchcraft only for the betterment of mankind, then Ally had no choice but to take matters into her own hands.

The sleepy southern town of Belhaven had been charitable enough to take in their kind hundreds of years ago and keep their witchcraft a secret from the rest of the world. The least *they* could do was adhere to the laws set in place and behave like respectable citizens. And being a respectable citizen did *not* mean spinning a giant spider web to catch the town men and have your wicked way with them.

No matter how naughtily delicious that sounded.

Selina's wicked stunts had gained the town's attention and earned her a banishment spell. Ally insisted she be the one to cast it, for Selina's own safety. The truth was, the two were very close. Selina had been there on the worst night of Ally's life, consoling her when Tanner Cage, the only man Ally had ever loved, stood her up on prom night and skipped town the next day. That closeness made the discovery of Selina's secret antics all the more shocking to Ally.

Ally pushed open the door and inched inside, fearing Selina would detect her presence and surmise her intentions before Ally had a chance to cast the spell. A moan sounded from the back bedroom, drawing her attention.

Ally followed the sound. She craned her neck and peered into the dimly lit room. What she saw frightened and intrigued her at the same time. Smack-dab in the middle of the room was a huge floor-to-ceiling web with a gorgeous, well-endowed man attached. Whacking a crop across her palm, Selina circled him, keeping a wide berth as she examined his rippled physique.

Selina turned at the sound of Ally moving into the room. She arched a delighted brow. "Hello, cousin. How nice of you to join me."

"I'm not here to *join* you, Selina."

"No?"

Fingering the packet in her pocket, Ally stepped closer. "You can't do this, Selina. It's wrong."

"Tsk . . . tsk . . . always the good witch, Ally." She slapped the crop harder against her palm and then pointed it at Ally. "I know deep inside there is a part of you that would love to have your very own toy like this." She waved her hand toward her naked captive. "Besides, look at that beast." She pointed to his erection. "He doesn't look too distraught to me."

Ally was pretty sure his girlfriend would be. "It's still wrong, Selina."

Selina chuckled. "Why don't you let your naughty little witch out to play once in a while?"

Ally grabbed the herbs from her pocket and sprinkled them into the air. A cloud of fog formed around Selina. Ally began to chant the banishing spell.

Selina's eyes opened wide. Her hands flew up in a halting motion. The crop fell to the floor. "Ally, no," she cried, her voice growing faint as Ally circled her and continued to recite the spell.

Ally sprinkled more herbs into the air. "I'm sorry, Selina, you gave me no choice. Believe me, I'm doing this for your own good."

Selina's skin grew translucent. Her gaze locked on Ally's. "I'll be back, Ally. Just wait and see . . ."

Those were the last words Ally heard before her cousin disappeared into the fog.

# ONE

*Ten years later*

*S*OMETHING WAS NOT RIGHT in the sleepy southern town of Belhaven.

Ally Shears placed a book on the gray metal shelf in front of her as a shiver of unease crawled over her skin like an insect. Every nerve ending in her body began tingling with foreboding and she knew—better than she knew every nook and cranny in the library she'd been working at for the past few years—that a dark cloud had descended over the town.

She felt a presence behind her. Ally spun around, half expecting to see her banished cousin hovering there. Instead, she gasped in surprise as the handsome Sheriff Devlin came charging forward. Startled by the anger in his eyes, she pressed a hand to her chest and took one small step backward, positioning herself behind a rack of books.

"Selina's back in town," he growled, his dark eyes narrowing to mere slits as he fisted his broad hands at his sides.

She didn't care for his accusatory look. Did he somehow think this was her fault? After all, she had been the one to cast the banishing spell years previous. She schooled her expression. "Yes, I know," she said, keeping her voice low, controlled. She'd felt Selina's presence all day but had hoped like hell she'd been mistaken.

He drew an impatient breath and leaned toward her, using his height to look down on her. "She was spotted sneaking out of the old abandoned house on Manor Drive."

Ally frowned. Why they hadn't torn down that decrepit old place was beyond her. Especially after they'd found all of those men captured in Selina's silken webs. Men she'd lured to the manor and done sexual things to. Things that had left the town's women reeling, and some of the town men, well . . . violated. As a good, law-abiding witch, Ally would never consider doing something so wicked.

The sheriff raked an impatient hand through his thick black hair. "We need you to go over there, check things out and cast another banishment spell." He gave an angry shake of his head. "One that will hopefully *take* this time," he grumped, his dark brows furrowing slightly as he glared at her.

Ally wove her fingers together and resisted the urge to spin her own web and secure the sheriff to it. For punishment only. She never had cared for the way he looked down his nose at her since "the trouble"—as it had become known around town.

She pushed Devlin's remarks to the back of her mind. Right now she needed to concentrate on the herbs required for the spell to send Selina back to the netherworld, for the good of the town as well as Selina. Ally certainly didn't want her cousin taunting and tormenting the decent people returning to Belhaven for their high-school reunion this week—the same people who had rightfully demanded her banishment in the first place.

Centuries ago, Ally's descendants had escaped the Salem witch trials and settled in the scarcely populated, sleepy little town of Belhaven, a place outsiders rarely visited. When word eventually leaked that the newcomers were witches, the townsfolk were prepared to burn them at the stake. But after the witches proved that they had healing powers and were able to cure the sick and help the wounded, the city council had allowed the witches to stay, and had sworn to keep them secret from the rest of the world, providing they followed very stringent rules and only used their craft for the good of the people.

They lived among the townsfolk for centuries, gaining respect and trust. Of course, during Ally's lifetime, witchcraft had become much more accepted, as Wicca was practiced by many throughout the world.

Life had been pleasant in their small community—until Selina decided to wield power for her own selfish needs. It became evident that she had an agenda of her own when she began breaking every rule put in place by the council. Spinning strong, sticky webs made from fine, silky threads, she captured the good men of Belhaven and used them for her own pleasure. Now Ally and the rest of her clan were suffering the repercussions of her cousin's self-indulgent acts. The council had hushed up the incident, knowing that, with the exception of Selina, the witches were all law-abiding folks. Unfortunately, many people no longer trusted them, going out of their way to avoid her kind.

Ally took a quick peek at her watch and noted it was nearing four o'clock. Deciding to check out early, she glanced at Devlin. "I'm closing up now. I'll head over there just as soon as I lock the door and gather some herbs for the spell." She tilted her head to look him in the eye. "Will you be accompanying me?" she asked with bright-eyed innocence, knowing full well that the thought of going inside the mansion made the sheriff shiver beneath his wide-brimmed hat.

Her smile stretched wickedly as she watched him squirm under her steady gaze. His jaw clenched. "You think you'll need me?" he asked in an unstable voice. Before he drove his hands into his front pockets she noticed them shake.

She shrugged. "I might. Of course, if you're afraid . . ."

He gave a quick shake of his head. His eyes flashed. "It's not that—"

Cutting him off, she folded her arms across her chest. "Well, what exactly is it then?" she asked, deadpan.

"I think I should keep watch from outside. To wait for Selina's return." His deep voice stammered.

When she smirked at him he blurted out, "I'm *not* afraid."

*Well, he should be afraid,* Ally mused, *because Selina had certainly had it out for him ever since he'd flatly turned her down, years ago. Lord knows what my cousin would do to him, given the opportunity. The last place Devlin wanted to be caught was in one of Selina's webs.*

Or *hers,* for that matter, if she ever decided to spin one.

Lucky for the town, Ally was a good witch.

# TWO

ALLY STOOD BACK AND EXAMINED the crumbling mansion, left abandoned for years. Ivy climbed the walls like snakes and coiled around the posts that supported the veranda. The grounds and walkway were overgrown with shrubs, weeds and wildflowers. With the sheriff remaining a good twenty feet behind her, she made her way onto the porch. Chips of old white paint peeled beneath her hand as she brushed her fingertips over the wooden railing leading up the steps.

When she reached the massive front entrance, she closed her fingers over the brass doorknob and pushed. The heavy door creaked open, the hinges moaning like a wounded animal. Ally looked over her shoulder and gave a curt nod to the sheriff, signaling she was going in.

She felt a sense of déjà vu as she squeezed the packet of herbs inside the front pocket of her jeans and took a tentative step inside the old house. The planked floorboards groaned beneath her. Every light footstep stirred the air. Small particles of dust rained down from the ceiling, dancing and shimmering in the long column of late afternoon sunlight that sliced through cracks in the decaying cedar siding.

The air smelled stale and pungent. Like day-old pizza and beer. Or socks that had been left in a gym bag too long. Ally crinkled her nose and concentrated on breathing through her mouth.

A murmur coming from the back of the mansion drew her attention. She quietly padded down the long, dark hallway until she stood outside a closed door. Pressing her ear to the wooden slats, she listened.

Silence.

She lowered herself onto her knees and peeked through the large keyhole. The sunshine slanting through the open window gave off sufficient light for her to see a man squirming, trying to break free from the strong, binding web that held him captive.

From ceiling to floor, a web had been spun in the center of the room. With his back clinging to the sticky strands, his hands were secured over his head. His long legs were spread wide apart and securely attached as well. With his head turned away from her, she couldn't discern his features. God, he was so big, like a Viking warrior. His presence swallowed up the small room.

She bit down on her bottom lip as she slowly perused the length of him. His thick, sculpted muscles bulged in all the right places and threatened to rip the seams of his snug jeans and short-sleeved shirt. She was actually quite surprised to find him still fully clothed. Selina obviously hadn't finished what she'd started.

Her gaze traveled over his unruly mass of dark hair and then lower, over his broad shoulders and tight abs, stopping only when she reached the apex of his legs. She swallowed hard. Oh *yes*, his muscles definitely bulged in all the right places. Whoever said good things come in small packages certainly wasn't talking about this guy. She stared at his impressive size for an endless moment as she undressed him with her eyes. Awareness started at her core and rippled onward and outward. Her whole body began tingling in the most interesting places. When she gave a sexy moan, he began to turn in her direction. As if she'd been caught with her hand in the cookie jar, Ally quickly pulled back from the keyhole and straightened. She brushed the dirt from her knees and took a fueling breath of courage before entering. She had no idea what else she was going to find behind that door.

When she closed her hand over the knob, a breeze from the open window stirred the air. Suddenly, a very enticing, very *familiar* smell seeped through the keyhole and reached her nostrils. She inhaled deeply as the spicy, manly scent sent her thoughts spiraling back in time.

Memories flashed through her mind like lightning. Memories of her senior prom and the handsome Tanner Cage, high-school heartthrob and captain of the football team.

She'd been so madly in love with him. She'd taken extra care in her appearance that beautiful spring evening, arranging her long golden curls on top of her head, letting a few tendrils spill down her neck, just the way he'd liked. Underneath her pale blue satin gown she'd worn a silky white chemise, knowing she was finally going to give her virginity to the man she loved.

The truth was, Ally had always loved Tanner. Since kindergarten, really. It wasn't until high school—when she'd traded her thick glasses for contacts, lost the braces and gotten curves in all the right places—that he'd begun to see her as something more than the neighborhood tomboy.

Tanner had asked her out during their senior year. After that first date, they became inseparable, joined at the lips, as some would say. They'd eagerly—and naïvely—talked about marriage.

A smiled touched Ally's mouth as she recalled his pet name for her. Ally Cat.

Tanner Cage had been her soul mate. Her everything. And she had been ready to take their relationship to the next level. They both wanted their first night together to be special and had agreed they would consummate their love on prom night. That night had never happened. He'd left her standing on her doorstep waiting for him. Ally had cried until the sun came up. The next day she heard Tanner had skipped town and joined the military. Ally had never set eyes on him again and the last she heard, he was doing an overseas tour of duty as a Navy SEAL.

Selina had stayed by her side, comforting her. Even though Selina had done wrong by the townsfolk, she'd always been there for Ally. They were family—blood sisters—which made it twice as difficult for Ally to banish her. But Ally knew the banishment was for Selina's own safety.

Tanner Cage had broken Ally's heart and destroyed her belief in happily ever after. She'd been with other men since that dreadful night, of course, but how could she ever connect with a man emotionally? How could she ever find true love or give her heart to another when it belonged to one man—a man who didn't want it?

She shook her head, clearing away her painful thoughts. She gave a heavy sigh, knowing that if she ever did set eyes on him again, she'd make him pay for that dreadful night. He'd be smart to spend his life steering clear of her. She knew the well-disciplined witch inside her was only so forgiving.

She twisted the knob, eased the door open and stepped inside the room. Her eyes widened in astonishment as she took in the vision before her. The sound of her indrawn breath filled the air. Her pulse drummed in her neck and she had to lock her knees to avoid collapsing. Faltering backward, she gripped the doorknob as if it were a lifeline.

When those beautiful, familiar green eyes met her gaze, the edges of her vision became fuzzy. Feeling lightheaded, she drew air into her lungs.

God, it couldn't be him. It just couldn't. Not after all this time.

His dark brows knitted together. "What do you want with me?" he asked, tugging hard on the binding threads. "And what the fuck is this thing I'm stuck to?"

Ally bit down on her lip. The truth was, he was better off not knowing.

When she didn't answer, he asked again, "What do you want with me?"

She remembered that deep voice. So rich and enticing. Like warm melted butter. It seeped into her skin and filled her with heated memories of his passionate touch, his fiery kisses. Heat curled inside her. She pinched her lips tight and suppressed a ragged moan.

Was it really him or was she just dreaming? Had that delectable, familiar male scent simply caused her mind to conjure up the image?

She narrowed her gaze. "Tanner?" she asked quizzically, seeking verification that the man from her past had suddenly resurfaced.

He glared at her, confusion obvious in his gaze. "Do I know you?"

She drew in a sharp breath. It *was* him. And he didn't remember her. She straightened her spine and swallowed. Perhaps he couldn't see her well in the dark shadows of the room. She took a tentative step closer, providing him with a better view of her face.

"It's me. Ally."

"Ally?" He paused as though searching his memory. "I don't know anyone by the name of Ally."

Her heart crumbled like the burnt toast she'd eaten for breakfast. How could he not remember her? They'd been in *love*. At least she had thought they were. Was she so forgettable that the man she'd wanted to spend the rest of her life with could so easily dismiss her from his memories?

Determined to get to the bottom of it, Ally searched for an explanation. "Do you have amnesia? Or memory loss? Did something happen during your last tour of duty?"

"No," he bit out. "You obviously have me mixed up with someone else."

Another thought struck her and made her stomach curdle. Had somebody played with his memory? Used witchcraft on him? The only one she knew who had ever abused the craft was . . . Selina.

She opened her mouth to ask, but shut it when he cut her off with a glare. She *had* to be mistaken. Selina and Ally had been more like sisters than cousins. She recalled the way Selina had spent the night comforting her when Tanner had run off. Ally refused to believe Selina would hurt her like this. Besides, Selina's wicked antics hadn't started until a few years after Tanner had left town.

Hadn't they?

"Are you going to let me down?" he asked.

"I *was* going to," she replied, walking over to the table beside him to look over the contents. Lubricant, a pink vibrator, nipple clamps, two long candlesticks and a book of matches. A leather crop drew her attention. How interesting. She picked it up and ran her hands over the long, textured length of it. She wondered what kind of fun Selina'd had with that particular prop.

His body stiffened with annoyance. "What do you mean, you were going to?" he bit out.

Silence ensued as she took a long moment to peruse the captive man before her. Gone was the thin teenage boy she'd fallen for. In his place was a man. A man with broad shoulders and thick, sculpted muscles. A man who oozed sexuality in a way the young, high-school boy never had.

"You know, Tanner, you owe me something." She stepped close—close enough that his scent overwhelmed her senses. Pressing the crop against his cheek, she let it slide over his neck, his chest and lower, until it grazed the huge bulge between his legs.

He flinched. His eyes darkened as disbelief marred his features. "How can I owe you anything? I don't even *know* you."

"That's where you're wrong. We knew each other quite . . . intimately," she murmured.

She watched his glance leave her face and wander down her body. He dragged his teeth over his bottom lip as his eyes latched upon her breasts. Ally felt her nipples harden involuntarily under his lusty gaze. Her chest heaved as a surge of blood rushed through her veins.

"Ally . . ." He let her name roll off his tongue as though he were testing it, tasting it. His gaze smoldered as it locked with hers. "If I'd known you . . . *intimately*," he said, lowering his voice, "there's no way in hell that I'd forget."

His warm breath caressed her face like a lover's kiss. Her body came alive, stimulated by his bold words. A tingle worked its way down her spine. She blinked and fought to recover her voice. "Well, it seems you did, now, doesn't it?" she challenged.

He gave her a sexy, predatory grin. "Why don't you let me down and give me a chance to sample that hot body of yours. Perhaps that will help trigger my memory." His voice dripped with sensual promise.

She slowly walked around him, dragging the long crop over his hard body. She felt his muscles bunch. She stopped directly in front of him and looked deep into his gorgeous eyes. A sudden surge of anger and hurt welled up inside her. "Or perhaps I could leave you here and make you pay for forgetting me."

He growled and struggled with the silken web. "You wouldn't!" His voice sounded whiskey-rough.

When their gazes met and locked, she expected to see rage. What she saw instead captivated her. Heat coiled deep in her belly as moisture gathered between her thighs. The passion that shimmered in his eyes made her breath catch and her anger recede. Her brain stalled and she had to remind herself to breathe.

"What exactly is it I *owe* you, Ally?" The deep timbre of his voice made her shudder.

"A prom night," she said and pressed the crop hard against his growing cock.

TANNER GROANED AND PRESSED into her touch. Fuck, that felt good. He had no idea who this woman was or what she thought he owed her, but if she kept touching him like that he was going to rupture an artery.

He thought back to his senior year and couldn't recall ever knowing an Ally. He wasn't sure why she had brought up the prom. He'd never even gone. Never planned to. He'd always thought of it as a senseless ritual. Instead, he had met up with the guys, knocked back a few beers and then left town to join the military.

Ally reached out and swept aside a lock of his hair. When she did, he watched color bloom high on her cheeks and wondered what she was thinking. Wondered what the hell she planned on doing with that whip she clutched in her tightly fisted hand.

His question was quickly answered when Ally drove the crop between his jean-clad legs and pressed the knobbed end between his ass cheeks. It stung, but he liked it. He bit down on his bottom lip and forced himself not to show his reaction. *Holy shit.* He could hardly believe how turned on he was. When his eyes locked with hers, he was both aroused and chilled from the intensity in her gaze.

If he'd had a sexy woman like her waiting for him at the prom, no way in hell would he have ever skipped town.

With a featherlight touch she skimmed her fingers over his

cheek, his lips and lower, until her hand hovered over the top button of his shirt. The feeling was erotically stimulating and every muscle in his body twitched. His heart began to pound beneath her touch.

Once again he racked his memory, trying to recall who she was. Nothing. Surely she was mistaken. Surely he didn't know her. His gaze traveled over her face. She was beautiful—exquisite, really—with honey-amber eyes and hair the soft golden color of a wheat field. Her full breasts narrowed to a slim waist that bloomed into curvy hips. Her long, sexy legs were wrapped in a pair of snug-fitting jeans. And she smelled so damn good. Like vine-ripened raspberries. Her feminine aroma was vaguely familiar, yet he couldn't quite put his finger on it. He inhaled deeply, letting her scent fill his senses.

He shook his head. There was no way he'd ever forget a woman as sexy as she was. No way in hell. *Especially* if they'd been intimate.

When his gaze settled back on the creamy swell of her heavy breasts, a tremor ripped through him. His mouth watered for a taste as his cock throbbed in response. He became acutely aware of how much his body ached for her touch.

She reacted to the tremor she felt in his body. Her fingers slipped from his chest and dropped to his cock. She cradled his erection in her delicate hand.

"Seems you might be a bit intrigued by my plan." Her sexy voice vibrated all the way down to his toes.

He swallowed and focused on what she was doing with her fingers. "What exactly *is* your plan?"

She gave him a sly smile. "If I told you, that would take the fun out of it, now, wouldn't it?" When she gently squeezed his balls, he growled and thrust his hips forward. Unfortunately, the silky web prohibited him from moving too far.

"Let's just say I think you need to be punished for breaking my heart and abandoning me on prom night. I missed out on a night of lovemaking with you that I'd been dreaming about all year." Mischief danced in her eyes.

"Let me down from here, Ally," he growled. "I mean it." When she ignored his protests he continued, "If you don't, you'll pay." Perspiration beaded his forehead.

She shook her head slowly. Her eyebrows raised a fraction. "No, I don't think so. I kind of like you this way." She began working the buttons on his shirt. "Besides, you're the one who's going to pay."

The determined look in her eyes heated his body. A tremor moved through him—from passion, not anger.

"I could yell for help." He twisted his right hand and was surprised to find he'd somehow managed to snap the seemingly unbreakable silken bindings. He hid that information from her.

"Yes, I suppose you could." Her voice was a hoarse whisper. She met his gaze straight on and moistened her lips. "If you wanted to," she challenged. The heat in her eyes licked over his body.

Giving up on the buttons, she grabbed his shirt and ripped it open. The buttons popped and sprinkled on the floor. She splayed her hands over his chest and leaned in until her mouth was a breath away from his. Her fingers toyed with his nipples. He sucked in a sharp breath and exhaled a groan.

She pitched her voice low. "Do you want to scream, Tanner?" There was a little erotic whimper in the back of her throat.

He clenched his jaw. Yes. No. *Fuck.* How could he possibly make a rational decision when all the blood was draining from his head and settling low in his groin?

She brushed her mouth lightly over his. Her hips bumped into his thighs. Her puckered nipples pressed into his chest. A tremor racked his body. He growled, pressed his lips hungrily into her sweetness and deepened the kiss with wild abandon. The heat from her mouth scorched his soul and stirred the fire inside him. Blood pounded through his veins. Needing to touch her, he struggled against the silky web. She tasted like sex and sin and heaven, all at the same time.

Suddenly he knew there was no way in hell he was going to yell for help.

# THREE

ALLY STEPPED BACK AND TOOK a moment to regroup. Her simple plan to arouse Tanner, leaving him unfulfilled and longing for more, the same way he'd left her many years ago, had suddenly become a little more complicated. His erotic kiss fueled her hunger and left her yearning for one of more substance. He was so beautiful, so muscular and so hard that her body came alive, just from looking at him.

The heat and energy radiating from his flesh stirred her libido. Warmth pooled in her pussy and filled her with a restless ache—an ache to feel skin against skin, to be kissed by his sensual lips, to be touched by his thick, capable hands and to feel his growing erection stoke the fire simmering inside her.

Without realizing what she was doing, she cupped her breasts, ran her thumbs over her protruding nipples and whimpered. Her eyes connected with Tanner's. The look on his face told her all she needed to know. Watching her pleasure herself excited him. She bit down on her bottom lip and considered that bit of information. Perhaps that could be part of her plan. To let him watch as she touched herself. To leave him hot and needy while she eased the mounting tension deep inside her slick pussy.

"Do you like this, Tanner?" Ally ran her fingers down her neck and dipped them under the thin fabric of her T-shirt. A shiver prowled through her body and turned her inside out as his burning eyes left her face and lingered on her breasts. Throwing her head back, she moaned in delight as her warm fingers connected with her tight peaks. A fever rose in her and she knew she had to find release before her entire body went up in flames.

"Let me fuck you, Ally," he murmured, the rough timbre in his voice giving way to soft persuasion.

She looked him square in the eyes. They were dark, full of lust. She sucked in a tight breath as her head began spinning. So tempting. So very, very tempting. She became hyperaware of the thick bulge between his legs. Her pussy moistened, urging her to give in to her desires. As much as she loved that idea, she knew that wasn't part of her plan. That would give *him* pleasure. Shaking her head to clear it, she fought her traitorous libido, reminding herself what he'd done to her.

Blowing out a shaky breath, she tried to keep the longing from her voice. "Why do I need you to fuck me, when I have this?" She walked over to the table and picked up the long, pink vibrator.

His nostrils flared. "Because my tongue can do things to you that that device can't."

For a brief moment she pictured his mouth buried deep inside the dark triangular patch at the apex of her legs. His tongue licking, sucking, nibbling, bringing her to previously undiscovered heights of ecstasy. Her whole body quivered as liquid desire dampened her panties.

She fought to find her voice. "Pretty sure of yourself, aren't you?"

"Yes," he growled with a touch of arrogance in his voice. "Let me down from here and I'll prove it."

When she shook her head back and forth he let out a roar of frustration. Dropping the rubber cock back onto the table, she closed the distance between them. She ran her hand down his smooth, tanned chest. His moist skin felt wonderful beneath her fingers. Her hand dropped to his waistband. She unfastened his button and listened to the hiss of his zipper as she drew it down. "Just to show you that I'm not totally insensitive, I thought I'd give your cock some breathing room. It does seem rather constrained behind your tight jeans."

After she freed his erection, it sprang out from its restrictive confines, clamoring for attention. Ally gasped in surprise as her pulse leapt in her throat. He was so big, so thick. The swollen purple head looked velvety soft. Her fingers tingled, anticipating a touch. Her mouth watered for a taste. Desire burned so hot in her she felt dazed. The need to touch him, to stroke her tongue over his smoothness, consumed her.

Raw, primitive urges took over, and before she realized what she was doing, she dropped to her knees. She moaned and pulled his cock into her hungry mouth.

She threaded her fingers through his silky curls and cupped his heavy balls. Rocking on her heels, she pumped his cock in and out of her slick mouth. She remained nestled between his legs for a long moment, her tongue stroking and laving his engorged shaft. Lust spread like wildfire through her body as she reveled in his taste.

His low growl of pleasure brought a smile to her face. It was easy to tell he was close to erupting. Her tongue urged him on. His balls tightened against his skin, his cock swelled in her mouth, liquid desire dripping from the tip. She pulled away, leaving him teetering on the edge.

"Don't stop, Ally. Please, not yet." His voice was harsh, rough. He thrust his hips forward in search of her mouth.

Ally stood on wobbly legs and met his gaze. She pouted her full lips. "It seems I've gone and wet my panties," she murmured.

He began panting heavily as she backed away and unsnapped her jeans.

She shook her hair from her face and presented him with a mischievous smile. "Perhaps I should take them off."

The heat in his eyes licked over her skin. "Yes, take them off. Take *everything* off," he blurted out as he struggled to free himself. "Let me see your cunt, Ally."

Ally seductively wiggled her backside as she slowly drew her pants over her thighs. Tanner's tortured curses reached her ears. "Fuck, Ally, what are you doing to me?"

She kicked her pants away and widened her legs. Desire twisted her insides as she dipped her finger inside her drenched panties. She drew in a tight breath as her nail grazed her inflamed clit. "Mmmmm . . ." she moaned, throwing her head back as she pleasured herself.

"I'm gonna fuck you if it's the last thing I do." His voice was a ragged whisper.

Ally paused and looked at him. His gorgeous green eyes were dark with heat—and promise.

"You can bet on it," he assured her. She bit down on her lip as a fine tingle of anticipation worked its way down her spine.

"Are you forgetting who's in control here?" She reached down and picked up the bright pink sex toy. Her eyes never once broke the steamy hold she had on him as she stroked her hand over the bulbous head. She drew it into her mouth and licked the tip, imagining it was his cock she was suckling.

Tanner's eyes tracked her every movement. His visual caress did mysterious things to her nerve endings. His nostrils flared as he clenched his jaw. She watched with heated interest as his chest rose and fell in a fast, erratic pattern.

Keeping her gaze locked on his, Ally took small steps, widening the distance between them, until her back was pressed against the wall. Drawing her panties down, she tossed them toward Tanner. They landed silently at his feet. Tanner's gaze dropped to her cunt. She positioned the rubber cock between her legs and opened her dewy folds, displaying the pink satiny skin of her most private flesh. "Is this what you wanted to see, Tanner?"

He gave a slow nod of his head and swallowed hard.

"You know—you could have had this on prom night if you hadn't run off," she murmured, lifting one leg and resting it on a nearby chair.

Tanner's jaw went slack, his eyes smoldering, and he was breathing as though he'd just run a marathon. He mumbled curses under his breath as he struggled to free himself.

In one smooth motion she breached her slick opening. The pink toy pushed against the walls of her tight pussy. She let out a long moan of pleasure as she savored the sensation. She slid the vibrator all the way into her slick core and back out again. Her liquid heat dripped over the rubbery head. All sense of time and place was lost on her as she worked the toy in and out of her heated channel and stroked her breasts with her other hand.

Blocking her mind to her audience of one, and concentrating only on her own pleasure, she pinched her eyes tight as she drove the thick rubber cock back inside her slick cunt. She was close, so close to finding release. Her breath came in ragged bursts as her orgasm neared.

"You're so sexy, baby." A rich, decadent rumble of pleasure sounded from the depths of his throat.

She loved the tone of his voice. So deep, so masculine. It seeped into her skin and filled her with a fiery need. She inhaled. His warm, masculine scent curled around her and urged her on. She pumped faster, harder, until she heard the dark whisper of his voice again. He sounded close. So close, in fact, she thought she felt his hot breath on her cheek. But that was impossible. He was trapped in Selina's web.

Her lids flew open. She'd been so lost in sensation, she hadn't realized Tanner had freed himself. She took a quick moment to appraise the situation, then made a move to run.

Using his body weight, he pinned her against the wall. She could feel his cock pressing against her midriff. "I'm about to make good on my promise," he breathed into her ear, his hands tracing the pattern of her curves. She shivered under his seductive touch.

She opened her mouth, but before she could say anything he closed his lips over hers. He moved his hand to the small of her back and drew her pelvis closer to him. He pulled the rubber cock from her pussy and tossed it aside. "You won't need that anymore," he growled into her mouth. He parted her swollen folds and eased three thick fingers deep inside her cunt while his thumb scraped over her clit.

Ally could barely summon the strength to remain standing. She sagged against him and he tightened his hold, bracing her to him. His gaze locked on hers as he worked her into a state of aroused euphoria. She wanted to push him away and run, but she couldn't. It felt too good, too right.

His lips greedily closed over hers and branded her with his heat. Twining her arms around his neck, she began panting heavily. He expertly fucked her with his fingers until she was on the brink of a powerful orgasm. She felt almost desperate for release. The desire in his eyes sent shivers through her body.

"Take your shirt off," he ordered. In one fluid motion she peeled it over her head and tossed it aside.

When his hungry gaze settled on her milky cleavage, her pussy began to clench. "That's it, baby. Let me finish what you started." She fell under the spell of his deep, mesmerizing voice.

Craving the feel of his skin, she pulled him against her naked flesh and began rocking her hips, meeting and welcoming his every thrust. She ran her hands over his thick, corded muscles, reveling in the feel of his moist flesh.

"Let me show you what my tongue can do." His voice thinned to a whisper.

She opened her mouth to speak but no words formed. His burning eyes left her face as he slowly tracked down her body. Settling himself between her legs, he urged her thighs wide open and lowered his head. She shivered with delight at the touch of his soft, velvety tongue.

"Sweet Jesus, Tanner!" she cried and arched her spine.

She moved against him restlessly and plowed her fingers through his hair. The pleasure he was giving her was beyond her wildest imagination. He did things to her body that no one had ever done before. Things that made her dizzy, wild, feverish. She wanted to touch him. Everywhere. She wanted her mouth on his chest, his abdomen, his cock. It was too much, too intense.

Scraping her nails over his shoulders, she pulled on him. "Stop . . . stop . . . God, don't stop," she begged, as he continued his mind-blowing erotic assault.

His tongue probed her soaked opening, then licked her all the way from front to back. A jolt of fire curled around her and she began to quake. In no time at all an explosion tore through her as she shuddered her surrender.

Tanner let out a low growl of satisfaction when her juices poured into his mouth. Wrapping his arms around her waist, he held her and absorbed her tremors as she took her time coming back down to Earth. After her breathing regulated he slid up her body until his mouth hovered over hers.

Her heart lurched in her chest as she watched him. Every old feeling she had for him came clawing back to the surface. She was still so deeply in love with him. But her emotions were quickly squelched when she recalled that he didn't even remember who she was.

"Now, wasn't that better than some toy?" he asked, his lips glistening with her desire. She could smell her heady scent on his breath.

Lowering her gaze to shadow the emotions in her eyes, she nodded. It occurred to her that the reason she'd kept him secured

to the web wasn't to make him pay for leaving her—it was with
the hope that he'd remember her, remember their past.

When he shifted closer, she felt the wet tip of his arousal
press against her. She began to feel guilty for trying to keep him
captive. Especially after he'd freed himself and given her such intense pleasure without taking anything for himself.

"I'm sorry," she murmured. "It was wrong of me to keep you
captive. Let me make it up to you."

He pulled her into his embrace, twisted them around and
began to walk her backward. "What exactly do you have in
mind?" he asked, a playful glint in his eyes.

She shrugged and nibbled on her lower lip. "I don't know.
Maybe dinner."

He chuckled softly. "I have a better idea." His deep voice
dropped to a whisper that caressed her body.

"Oh? And what would that be?" she asked tentatively, watching his thick muscles shift with each movement.

"Tell me more about this prom night we missed. What was so
special about it? What were we going to do?" A warm smile
turned up the corners of his sexy mouth and softened his features.

When she lowered her head, he cupped her chin and tilted
her face until their eyes locked. "Tell me," he coaxed softly.

The tenderness in his voice made her blurt out the truth.
"We . . . we were going to make love. You were going to be my
first."

Wrapping his arms around her waist, he effortlessly picked
her up and pushed her shoulder blades against the sticky web,
trapping her.

Her eyes opened wide in surprise as the strong bindings secured her in place. "What . . . what are you doing?" she cried, alarm obvious in the tone of her voice. She felt her face go pale as she hopelessly struggled to free herself.

He picked up the leather crop and looked deep into her eyes. "I'm going to give you the prom night you never had."

THE AIR IN THE ROOM HAD COOLED considerably as night approached. Neither one of them seemed bothered by the chill as their desire kept them hotter than the inside of a furnace. The sun had disappeared over the horizon, leaving the room draped in darkness. Tanner shut the window and lit the candles on the side table. The warm flickering light silhouetted their bodies.

He took a small step back and perused the naked woman before him. The soft glow of the candlelight made her honey-gold skin glisten. By God, she was exquisite. It wasn't just her physical appearance that attracted him. There was something about her. Something that drew him in and tugged at his emotions. She was unlike any other woman he'd ever been with. In fact, she was everything he'd ever been looking for. How could he not remember her? Ally's voice pulled him back to the situation at hand.

"Let me down from here," she demanded, her eyes flashing with anger and something else. If he had to guess, he'd say passion, anticipation.

He stepped closer, until he could feel the heat radiating from her body. Using the backs of his fingers, he trailed a line down her face. Her skin felt so soft beneath his hand. Looking at her made him wild with the need to fuck her. She stiffened and twisted her head sideways, breaking his touch.

She glared at him and blew out a shaky breath. "The sheriff is outside waiting for me. I could scream." Her voice rose an octave.

He smiled and skated a finger over the milky curve of her breasts. He could feel her heart pounding inside her chest. His fingers dropped to her cunt and threaded through the fine hair between her thighs. He caressed her nether lips and parted her folds. His fingers quickly became drenched with her moisture. When he wiggled his finger, she arched into him and bit down on her bottom lip. Her action was so telling. She was excited. That pleased him.

"Yes, you could," he said, his voice rough. "If you wanted to," he challenged.

"Of course I want to," she said, her cheeks turning one shade pinker. He watched her throat as she swallowed.

His grin widened as he lightly massaged her engorged clit. "Now, why would you do that, Ally? Why would you deny yourself what you really want?"

She opened her mouth and he silenced her with a kiss. He pressed his lips over hers. Hard. Possessively. He traded hot, wet kisses with her for a long, endless moment, until his touch penetrated her defenses. Soon her lips widened and her tongue moved inside to mate with his. Every sensual movement of her body indicated her wants and desires.

He let out a low growl of longing as he began to devour her with his mouth. He pressed his cock against her, letting her know the effect she had on him. When she began whimpering for more, he buried his face in the side of her neck. He lingered there, breathing in her erotic scent.

His cock throbbed painfully, screaming for release. But he wasn't about to give in to his need just yet. First he wanted to drive this luscious naked woman beyond the brink of sanity. He wanted to stir the fire in her until she begged for release.

"Please, Tanner, more. I want more." She squirmed and tossed her head to the side. "I want to feel you inside me."

A sound rumbled deep in his throat. "Ah, now it's *you* who begs." Dropping the crop he still clutched in one hand, he quickly discarded his pants and removed his shirt. His hands gripped her hips and held her pelvis close to his. His cock scraped her swollen clit. Her sigh of sweet pleasure filled the room.

He twisted his head and examined the items on the table beside him. The candlelight flickered across the ceiling, creating shadows and providing him with enough light to examine the sex toys on display.

His blood began racing with anticipation. "What do we have here?" he asked, stepping away to grab the nipple clamps. "Were you planning on using these on me?"

She shook her head as her eyes lit up with apprehension. "No. Those aren't mine."

He turned the clamps over in his hands and smiled at her. Ally's chest began to rise and fall quickly. "Tanner . . ." Her voice was a hesitant whisper.

"Shhhh." He pressed a finger to her lips.

She swallowed her protests when he bent forward and licked the creamy valley between her heavy breasts. A bead of perspiration trickled down her chest and he leaned in and tracked it with his tongue. Her soft moan of pleasure reached his ears. He took one hard nipple between his lips and grazed his teeth over the delicate flesh. Drawing the rock-hard nub deeper into his mouth, he suckled until hollows pulled at his cheeks. He felt her go wild under his gentle assault. She took deep gulping breaths as he treated her other nipple to the same erotic pleasure. Before she had time to protest further, he attached the nipple clamps to her breasts.

Pitching forward, her eyes opened wide in surprise. She moistened her lips and gasped. By small degrees her expression changed from apprehension to excitement. "Tanner that feels . . . I don't know. It hurts, but it feels incredible at the same time." He pulled on them just a little and she whimpered.

Tanner grabbed the crop and began dragging it over her quivering flesh. "You've been a naughty girl, Ally. What made you think you could keep me captive and torture me by making me watch you pleasure yourself? Didn't you think there would be consequences?" When she didn't answer he pulled on the nipple clamps. "I asked you a question," he growled.

Her head lolled to the side. "I . . . I don't know." He watched her lids flicker as her eyes darkened with desire.

Tanner circled around her. Reaching down, he used all his strength to tear the bindings around her lush backside, giving him access to her most intimate areas. He pulled apart her perfectly sculpted, heart-shaped ass cheeks. She clenched her pink puckered hole. He stroked the tender flesh with the tip of his finger and she squirmed. Careful to avoid the web, he put his lips close to her ear and whispered, "Naughty girls must be punished,

Ally." He pushed one long finger into her tight opening. Her heat curled around him like a glove.

"Tanner . . ." she whimpered, her voice merely a breathless whisper.

Something in her voice was so comforting, so familiar. It seeped inside him and filled him with warmth. A rush of feelings exploded through him and left him shaken. He was unprepared for the onslaught. In that instant, he knew what he felt for her was more than just a sexual pull. He also knew how easily it would be to lose himself, heart and soul, in this sweet, sexy, *amazing* woman.

Her head rolled to the side. "Tanner," she whispered again as he worked his finger inside her. God, he loved the way she said his name.

It amazed him how important her pleasure had suddenly become to him, and how deeply they'd connected on an intimate level. Tanner wanted nothing more than to give her a wonderful experience, a "first time" experience that she'd never had with another man.

The sudden image of her with another man filled him with an unexpected rage. What the hell was going on with him? He couldn't explain it—couldn't explain all the muddled feeling and emotions churning inside him. All he knew was he wanted to be her first for a lot of things. Her first *and* her last. If another man touched her, he just might have to kill him.

# FOUR

ALLY HAD NEVER FELT ANYTHING quite like Tanner's finger probing her ass. It was both pain and pleasure mingled into one. When she wiggled her backside, Tanner growled and pushed his finger in deeper.

"Tell me, Ally. Have you ever been fucked here?" He pulled his finger out, spread her cheeks wider, and rubbed the crop over her swollen opening.

She shook her head and gasped for her next breath when the crop breached her ringed passage.

"Since I supposedly stood you up on prom night and missed being your first here"—he reached around and fondled her pussy—"then perhaps I can be your first *here*." He coaxed the crop in another inch.

He grabbed the bottle of lubricant off the table and poured a generous amount into his hand. "How does that sound, Ally? Do you want me to be your first?"

"Tanner, I don't think . . ." Her words trailed off when he withdrew the crop and his slick finger reentered her ass.

"I'll make it good for you, Ally. I promise," he whispered, easing in deeper.

She cried out and bucked against him. "Oh God, that feels incredible." Arching her back, she granted him deeper access. He worked his finger inside her for a long time, until she got used to the new feeling. She thought she was going to go mad with desire. The barrage of sensations made her body convulse. Suddenly it wasn't enough. She wanted more—*all* of him inside her.

"Please put your cock in me," she begged, ramming her ass harder against his finger. Her pussy dripped with desire. The scent of her arousal began to permeate the room, bringing her passion to new heights.

She could hear his breathing change and knew he was fighting for control. "No. First you'll fuck the crop until you get used to the feel." Even though he tried to sound harsh, she detected gentleness and caring in his voice. His tone softened. "Then maybe I'll let you have my cock." His words touched something deep inside her and stirred her emotions. She suspected she knew the real reason he didn't give her what she begged for. Taking her comfort and well-being into consideration, Tanner knew his impressive thickness would be too much for her to bear her first time.

She bit down on her bottom lip and fisted her hands above her head when he slathered her opening with warm lubricant. He eased the long crop inside her. She let out a little gasp as it filled her. Closing her eyes, she concentrated on the tiny points of pleasure. Her body began to tremble from the stimulation.

"You're so fucking hot, Ally. My cock is throbbing watching you take the crop into your ass." His voice caressed her flesh.

She had no idea being penetrated this way could be so pleasurable. Tanner seemed to know just what to do and just how to touch her. The sensual hunger he aroused in her was shocking. It was a pure carnal delight. She emitted a deep primal sound from the depths of her throat. She felt the muscles in her cunt begin to quiver.

His breath was hot on her neck. "Are you enjoying this, Ally? Do you like me being the first here?" he tenderly whispered into her ear, concern evident in his tone.

She couldn't find her voice to answer. Her throat was too tight with emotion. Instead, she arched her back, driving the crop in deeper. Tanner's hand slid over her hips and parted her labia. When he feathered his finger over her clit, she felt herself explode into a million fragments. Her head thrashed side to side as she tumbled into a powerful orgasm.

He eased the crop out and gently ran a soothing finger over her sensitive tissue. "I think your ass has had enough for today." He circled around her until they were eye to eye. He removed the nipple clamps and tossed them aside. "I didn't hurt you, did I?"

God, the compassion and concern in his eyes warmed her all over.

She shook her head from side to side and tried to recapture her breath. "No. It was perfect," she whispered, surprised that she was able to find her voice.

He reached down and stroked her slick cunt while his gaze settled on her mouth. "You're so wet, Ally. Do you know what that does to me?"

Aching to caress his face, she tugged on the binding strands, hoping to snap them. "It's what you do to me, Tanner. It's never been like this for me before. It's never been this good," she blurted out.

He furrowed his brow, aware of the emotions surging through him. "Why, Ally? Why is it so good with me?"

He watched her eyes turn glossy as she lifted her gaze to his. "Because I love you. I've never stopped loving you, Tanner." Her voice ended on a soft whisper.

He jerked his head back, his jaw dropping open. She lowered her lashes, shadowing her eyes.

Tanner nudged her chin up with his thumb. "It's never been this good for me before either, Ally," he admitted. He gave her a warm smile. "Sex has always just been about physical pleasure to me, but you make me feel something in here." He pressed his hand over his heart, then leaned forward and gave her a gentle, tender kiss on her forehead. "I don't know why. Honestly, I don't *know* you well enough to have feelings for you. But I *do* have feelings. Strong feelings." He shook his head. "I can't explain it to you because I barely understand it myself."

There was so much emotion in his voice it took her breath away. Ally felt her heart do a somersault while her stomach did cartwheels. She drew in a shuddery breath and absorbed the heat radiating from his body.

He ran his fingers up her arms until his hands locked with hers. His mouth hovered over her lips. She could feel his cock throb against her body. "Tell me how you like it, baby. Do you like it hard and fast or soft and slow?"

The fire in his eyes began burning her up. "It doesn't matter, Tanner. All that matters is that it's you who is giving it to me."

He grew quiet for a moment and then said, "Do you really love me?" His expression was bewildered, his voice full of disbelief.

A surge of warmth flooded her veins and she had a hard time

filling her lungs. "I've never loved anyone but you, Tanner." Her voice trembled. "When you ran away, you took my heart with you."

He cupped her face as his mouth closed over hers for a deep, passionate kiss. She felt his thick cock probe her opening.

"Please, Tanner. Let me down from here. I need to hold you in my arms again, just one more time."

With a quick, forceful tug he tore the silky bindings from her hands and pulled her to him. She collapsed against a wall of packed muscle. Burrowing her face in the crook of his neck, she inhaled his familiar scent while focusing on his touch and the feel of his skin against hers.

He gathered her into his arms and backed her up against the wall. Her body fit perfectly against his. She instinctively wrapped her legs around his back. "Fuck me, Tanner."

"No," he said. His gaze was powerful, unguarded.

She looked at him questioningly. Her brows knitted together as she frowned. "No?" Need made her voice husky.

He trailed a kiss over her jaw and looked at her with pure desire. "No, baby. I'm going to *make love* to you. The way you said we were supposed to years ago." There was such tenderness in his gaze.

Her pulse leapt in her throat. Ally twined her arms around his neck and pulled him closer. Her breasts pressed against his chest. She couldn't seem to get him close enough. She cried out his name as he pushed his thick cock into her. With slow, steady strokes he massaged the tight walls of her pussy, drawing out her pleasure.

"You feel amazing," he murmured into her mouth. His voice

covered her like a warm blanket as he filled her with his heat. When she squirmed against him, he pumped harder and faster. She could feel his cock throbbing inside her.

"Tanner . . . *please.*" Her voice quivered as she cried out to him. In her haze of arousal she had no idea what she was begging for. She only knew she needed him to ease the escalating tension building inside her.

She squeezed her cunt muscles around his cock. "Mmmm . . ." he moaned against her skin.

Reaching between their bodies, he pressed his fingers over her swollen clit, coaxing her body into release. Waves of pleasure began washing over her.

She threw her head back and gasped. "Don't stop," she whimpered as her release approached.

"I don't ever plan on stopping. Not today, not tomorrow, not next week. I'll never stop making love to you, Ally."

His words sent her over the edge. Her pussy began to spasm. She arched against him, drawing his cock deeper inside. She called his name and gasped in pleasure when his fingers caressed her sensitive flesh.

He lowered his head and drew her nipple into his mouth. The feel of his warm lips closing over her breast was exquisite. Her body shook as he laved her tight peak with his tongue. She went wild in his arms. She scraped her nails over his back and came apart completely. She felt Tanner's release shudder through him as he slammed into her and pinned her back to the wall.

He closed his mouth over hers and drew her in for a soul-searching kiss. She remained pressed against him until their hearts and bodies fused into one.

Tanner broke the kiss and finger-combed her hair off her face. He gave her a warm smile. He opened his mouth to say something but then shut it again. He looked perplexed. She looked into his eyes, searching for answers, but all she saw was unanswered questions.

"What is it?" she asked.

He gave a slight shake of his head. "Nothing." She was astonished by the tenderness in his voice.

Ally suspected she knew what he was thinking. "Why is it you can't remember me? Remember *us*?" Once again, Ally's stomach curdled, wondering if witchcraft was indeed involved. But who would do this to him? To her? And why?

Tanner shook his head sadly. He didn't have an easy answer. "I'm not sure."

"Well, well . . . What do we have here?"

# FIVE

ANNER AND ALLY BOTH SPUN around at the sound of the voice. When Tanner spotted a shadow in the dark corners of the doorway, he hooked his arm around Ally's waist and positioned her behind him. A moment later a beautiful woman stepped into the room. He vaguely recognized the girl with the long black hair and shimmering sapphire eyes. A knot tightened in his gut as he stared at her. There was something about her eyes. Something hauntingly familiar. Something . . . hypnotizing.

She stepped closer and slowly walked over to the table that held the used sex toys. The light from the flickering candle cast shadows across her porcelain profile. She twisted around to face them and pouted. "Seems I'm a little late for the party."

Tanner heard a small gasp escape from Ally. She grabbed him by the shoulder and whispered in his ear. "I need my pants."

He quickly scooped Ally's clothes off the floor and handed them to her. She hurried into her pants and pulled on her T-shirt. Tanner shrugged on his own shirt and climbed into his jeans.

"Do I know you?" he asked, widening his stance as though prepared for battle.

As soon as the girl smiled, it hit him. She was the one who had captured him. The last thing he remembered before Ally had come to his rescue was having a conversation about the Belhaven high-school reunion.

Tanner blinked and shook his head, trying to remember what had happened before he'd woken up bound to the web. He broke out in a cold, uncomfortable sweat. "What did you do to me?" he growled. He listened with one ear to Ally's low whispered chant behind him. What in the hell was she doing?

The dark-haired girl emitted a deep, sultry laugh from the depths of her throat. "Well, it seems I didn't get a chance to do *anything* to you. It looks like my lovely cousin got to you first."

Tanner spun around and glared at Ally. "*Cousin?* You were in on this?"

Ally shook her head, then glared at the dark-haired witch. "Selina's responsible for this, not me."

Tanner stepped back and shook his head. "Would somebody *please* tell me what's going on here?"

They ignored him and glared at each other.

"Selina, what are you doing? Why are you back in town? And why would you do this to Tanner?" Ally asked, her voice rising with each question.

Selina folded her arms across her chest and grinned. "Now, what kind of greeting is that, little cousin?"

"How did you get here?"

Selina's grin widened. "Bad *always* prevails over good, Ally. Haven't you learned that by now? I managed to find a way around your *ancient* banishment spell." She rolled her eyes. "As you know, I had many years to work on it."

*Banishment spell.* Tanner wrestled with half-forgotten memories. They were *witches?*

Ally slipped her hand into the front pocket of her jeans. "What do you want with Tanner?"

Selina's eyes darkened to black coals. Her jaw twitched. "Why do you care? He never loved *you.* If he had, he wouldn't have made love to me on prom night before he deserted you and joined the military."

Tanner watched Ally's shoulders stiffen. She shook her head in disbelief. "You were with me on prom night, Selina," she countered.

"Before that, cousin. While you stood on your porch and waited for Tanner, he was making love to me."

Face red with anger, Ally took a step toward Selina, but Tanner held her back. "He never would have done that," Ally bit out.

"If you don't believe me, ask him yourself."

Ally's mouth twisted as though she'd just sucked on a lemon. "I can't. It seems he's lost all recollection of that night. All recollection of *me* and the love we shared."

Tanner's head bobbed back and forth as he tried to follow the conversation. Tried to put together the pieces of the puzzle.

A mischievous grin curled Selina's lips.

Ally let out a humorless laugh and shook her head in disgust. "I can't believe you're responsible for this. Why, Selina? Why would you delete Tanner's memories? Why would you do this to him? To *me?*" she asked in a low, deceptively calm voice.

Like a bow stretched to the limit, Selina's composure snapped. She took a step forward and reached for something in her pocket. Tanner fisted his hands and waited. He wasn't about to let anything happen to Ally.

"He would have wanted me if *you* hadn't come along. Little Miss Perfect with a sweeter-than-sugar smile. The little tomboy who grew into a gorgeous cheerleader with all the popular friends. While I sat at home alone with no one."

Ally's eyes softened. "But you had me. And I thought we had each other."

Selina huffed. "We had *each other*? Are you forgetting you banished me to the netherworld?"

"Only for your own good, Selina. What you were doing to the townsfolk was wrong, and you know it. If they had gotten their hands on you before I sent you away, it could have been a lot worse. I was protecting you."

"I didn't need or want your protection, Little Miss Good Witch. Didn't you ever think I would tire of being in your *perfect* shadow?" Selina waved her hand through the air and snarled. "But I fixed you, *all* the women of Belhaven who preferred your friendship over mine and all men who never gave me the time of day. I made everybody in this town *pay* for overlooking me."

Ally stepped forward. "The townsfolk will pay no more for your imagined insults," she assured her.

In a motion so fast it took Tanner off guard, Ally pulled a packet out of her pocket and sprinkled the contents over Selina. Keeping a wide berth, Ally circled her cousin and began chanting a spell.

Selina laughed. "Oh please, little cousin. Your magic has grown weak from lack of use." Reaching into her own pocket, Selina pulled out a vial. "Now it's time for *you* to go visit the netherworld. And *you* won't be coming back." Selina glanced at Tanner. "But don't worry, Ally. I promise to take extraspecial care of *him*."

Ally twisted around and glanced at Tanner. "Get out of here now, while you still can."

"I'm not going anywhere without you, Ally. Ever again."

A movement at the door drew their attention. Tanner turned and spotted the sheriff.

Selina's eyes widened in delight. "*Sheriff*," she purred. "How nice of you to join us. Don't worry, I have something *extra-special* planned for you. No one turns me down without paying for it."

The sheriff drew his gun. Selina threw her head back and laughed. In that split second, Tanner lunged for her and knocked her off balance.

The vial flew into the air. Before it hit the floor and smashed, Ally grabbed it.

She pulled the rubber stopper free. "Tanner, *move!*"

As soon as Tanner distanced himself, Ally threw the potion on Selina and once again recited the spell.

A thick fog covering her, Selina cried out and lunged for Ally, but before she could grab hold, her body turned translucent. "I'll be back, Ally. Wait and see . . ."

"Not this time, you won't." Ally brushed her palms together. "You were wrong, dear cousin. Good *always* prevails over evil." She turned to the sheriff.

He scratched his head and gave her a genuine smile. "Thank you, Ally." Taking his notebook from his pocket, he turned. "This place gives me the creeps. I'll meet you both outside." His boots pounded the floor as he hurried outside.

Suddenly, as though he'd been struck by a wrecking ball, Tanner flew backward and hit the wall. He cracked his head and winced in pain. When he opened his eyes and looked up, Ally was standing over him. Her eyes were full of worry. She knelt down and brushed his hair off his forehead.

"Tanner, are you okay?" Her voice trembled. "Please be okay, my heart couldn't take losing you again."

Tanner looked deep into Ally's eyes as old memories flooded him. "Ally Cat," he said softly and pulled her down onto the floor with him.

Her relief was obvious. "Oh my God, Tanner, you remember." Her voice caught on a sob as tears pooled on her lashes.

He shook his head and smiled. "Your spell must have broken the one Selina had over me." He pulled her into his arms and she molded herself against him. Every forgotten emotion he'd ever had for her filled his heart. His insides ached with the love that overcame him. "I never slept with her, Ally. She tried to lure me into her bed, but I turned her down. That must be why she cast a spell over me and erased you from my memory."

"It's okay, Tanner. I believe you."

He cupped her chin and lifted her face until her eyes met his. "Baby, we've lost so much time together. I'm so sorry this happened."

"I know. Me too." The sadness in her heart was apparent.

He brushed her tears from her cheeks. "I love you, Ally Cat."

She closed her hand over his and sniffed. "I love you too, Tanner," she echoed. "I've never stopped."

He pulled her impossibly closer and she melted against him. "I always felt like there was something missing from my life, and now I know what it is. I want to make love to you every day for the rest of our lives to make up for all the lost time." He tilted his head to kiss her.

She inched her head back and looked at him. "One question." A sudden gleam sparkled in her eyes.

"What is it?" he asked, nuzzling her neck, inhaling her rich female scent.

"When do we start?"

# SOLO
# TU

## MANDY M. ROTH

## Dedication

To my editor, Nick Conrad, for putting up with my requests for men in loincloths fanning me and for making sense of the mess I call me. You helped bring Dante and Francy to life. Thank you for that and so very much more. Working with you has been a joy. Here's to many more projects in the future.

To the ladies who meet me for breakfast each and every morning and who aren't afraid to crack a whip. Mostly because they know I like it. And to Shane, who let me practice some of the angles to be sure they were right. Research is such a hard job, isn't it, honey?

# ONE

RANCY MONTGOMERY PULLED her silver sedan to a stop outside the three-story cream-colored home and killed the engine. It was strange being back after so long, but it was necessary. A strange calm surrounded her as she stared up at the house her longtime friend Dante insisted wasn't a mansion. With nine bedrooms and ten bathrooms, it counted as one in her book. Trust Dante not to think so. The man had been born in the lap of luxury.

Getting out of her car, she took in a deep, fresh breath of country air. The very sight of the place took her breath away. It was both overwhelming and exhilarating to see it again. Part of her wanted to get back in her car and drive away. Another part wanted to lay down roots and never leave again. Unfortunately, she couldn't do that. Running wasn't an option either.

Letting her power rise, Francy let it run out and over the grounds in search of Dante. A witch by birth, she had only learned to control her powers in the last several years. Being under thirty years of age made her a fledgling in the eyes of the supernatural world. Her lack of control and five-year span of trying to harness her powers was unacceptable by many, but not Dante. He made controlling supernatural gifts look simple and always made her feel good about what she'd accomplished. The minute she sensed his magik, Francy drew hers back quickly. Her entire body tingled from the rush of power and from the thrill of having brushed against Dante, even if it was only mystically.

*I should have just called. I can't face him.*

It had been over five years since she'd been able to visit Dante and she wasn't sure what to expect. Sure, they kept in touch as much as they could on the phone but they both led very busy lives. With the bombshell she had to drop on him, she was positive that their days of doing their best to stay in contact were numbered. Still, it was important that he hear the news she had to share before anyone else told him.

Rows of red tulips flanked the circular limestone drive, giving the illusion of a red-carpet welcome. The arched, notched-out entranceway had potted plants on it, consisting mostly of ivy. Italian herbs were randomly growing throughout as well. That suited Dante.

The plants softened the hard edges of the entranceway perfectly. Francy could still remember Dante planting them. She had been in high school, visiting her family's cottage, and he'd seemed desperate to find things to do to occupy his time. After all, the man had centuries under his belt and countless more to come. Immortality had its price—boredom seemed to be part of it.

*Desperate for anything to avoid one-on-one time with me.*

It was a harsh thing to think and not entirely true. So much had transpired between them that it was hard to pinpoint what they had. In her mind and her heart, she would always hold

Dante near—love him with more of herself than she would ever offer another. In reality, he was her friend. Nothing more. And now she was promised to another. That in itself was something she was coming to terms with.

Francy didn't bother knocking. It wasn't something she was known for when it came to visiting Dante, and it would seem time hadn't changed the habit. She opened the heavy wooden door and smiled when she found the front-room hearth covered in fruits and vegetables. It was an open layout, leaving the hearth in close proximity to a large wash basin. It was Dante's stopping spot from the garden. Francy could still picture him spending time cleaning all that he brought in from the garden in preparation for whatever feast he was planning.

She smiled as she stared at the hearth. The charred backdrop made her laugh as she remembered how and why it was that way. Stepping closer to it, Francy put her hand out, almost touching the scorch marks. The marks had been made when they had decided to enjoy a late-night meal together with a soothing fire going. Dante had insisted on cooking for her and there was no way she'd ever pass that up. Not with as excellent a chef as he was. His ability to turn ordinary pasta into something extraordinary had always won her over.

*The way to your heart, Francy, is through your stomach.* Dante's words echoed in her mind.

Francy let out a soft laugh at the thought of her friend's comment and how he would tease her that he had but to cook and she'd forgive him for just about anything. In truth, it wasn't quite that easy. There were things she wasn't sure she'd ever forgive him for.

Staring at the charred wall, she thought back to five years ago, when she'd last seen Dante. The meal had started out like any other but had ended in a way she'd never dreamt possible—with the two of them teetering on the edge of making love. They had come so close yet hadn't completed the act. It was a regret she would forever live with.

So many nights, when she should have been thinking of another, she'd lain in bed touching herself. Making herself come with the use of her fingers and memories of her night with Dante.

That night, Francy had been so aroused, so in need of Dante to be in her, fucking her, taking her every way possible, that she'd been careless with the gifts she'd been born with, accidentally releasing her magik and sending a charge into the fireplace. A second before Dante was about to slide his long, thick cock into her, huge flames shot forth, charring the cream-colored stone wall. It had left the two of them in an awkward spot, lying on his kitchen table, staring at the wall, and ended what could have been the beginning of something else entirely.

Francy still wasn't sure what Dante's reasoning was for casting her aside, telling her to go and live her life, but she did know that she'd never truly gotten over it. The odds were against that ever happening. Various scenarios had raced through her head but the best she could come up with was he didn't feel the same for her as she felt for him.

She had left town shortly after and hadn't been home since. Sure, Dante had spent years trying to convince her to return home, accept his apology and all would be right. Nothing was ever that easy. Francy had let someone else enter the equation but wasn't exactly sure why. She had felt compelled, as though a greater force was driving her, pushing her to accept another and move on.

"I can't believe he left the wall like that."

"And I," a deep, familiar voice said from behind her, "can't believe you're finally here. *Come sei bella*—how beautiful you are." The very sound moved over her, caressing her body in places it shouldn't be able to touch.

"Dante." Turning, she found him leaning against the entranceway. His onyx-colored hair came to his chin, perfectly framing his rectangular face. It swept out a bit, always looking as though it was windblown. Though he looked to be in his mid to late twenties, he was much older than that, two hundred years to be exact. Their age difference had bothered him once. He swore each time they spoke on the phone that it was no longer a concern, but with Dante she wasn't certain.

*He is gorgeous.*

Dante's dimpled chin and full lips had always been a source of fascination for her. Countless nights she'd lain in the cottage just beyond the edge of his property line with her hand buried between her legs, tweaking her clit to images of him.

*Stop thinking about him that way. You have someone else in your life now.*

He shifted slightly, causing the unbuttoned thin white cotton shirt he had on to move to one side. The sight of his steely, tawny chest and torso left her channel moist and her breathing ragged. The bulge in his khaki-colored, just-past-knee-length cotton drawstring shorts only served to make her moan softly. It didn't matter how many years she put between face-to-face visits, the man still made her body burn. If only he felt the same way.

*No. It's better he doesn't. You're with another man. Remember that.*

"Hey, you," she whispered with a smile on her face. Her pussy was damp and she could only hope that he couldn't smell it. The werewolf part of him had an uncanny ability to smell things mortals couldn't.

Dante's lips curved upward and Francy had to fight the need to run to him. "Are you planning on standing there all day or do I actually get a hug?"

"Gee, I don't know." She tipped her head and bit her lower lip. Every ounce of her wanted to tackle him. She somehow managed to maintain her tiny grasp on her self-control. "The last time I saw you, you were a real ass."

The warm laugh that trickled from his lips seemed to wrap around her, caress her in tender places. "You won't let me live that down, will you? I've spent five years apologizing to you."

"On the phone but not in person."

Dante moved quickly, covering the distance between them, and towered over her. His six-foot-two-inch frame was a sharp contrast to her five-foot-five one. Something about that had always appealed to her. He made her feel safe, protected at all times, and she was fairly sure that her smaller stature did something for him as well.

The minute his hands went to her exposed waist, resting between the stop of her mid-length white lace camisole and the start of her floor-length white silk chiffon skirt, her breath caught. Only Dante made her feel so alive with nothing more than his touch. Only Dante made her body ache to the point she had to fight the urge to beg him to take her.

*Why? Why can't I stay detached? I'm only here to mend fences, make peace and move on with my life. Nothing more.*

He traced tiny circles on her exposed flesh, driving her mad with lust. "Francy, I am so sorry. I lost my temper; chased you off. It will never happen again."

"What? You losing your temper or making me run away?" she asked without thought.

A sly smile broke over his face as he dipped his head down a bit. "You are the only woman I know who would think to have me clarify that."

Francy stared into his dark brown eyes and gave him a smug look. "I know you well enough to question anything you say, Dante."

"Do you now?" He planted a tiny kiss on the tip of her nose, shocking her into silence. Chuckling, he repeated his action before capturing her lips with his own. Fire shot through her.

Too stunned to move, Francy simply stood there, allowing Dante to taste her. Her mind screamed at her to stop what was going on, to make him get away, but her body burned for him to be closer. It was intoxicating to have his warm tongue sliding into her mouth. It greeted hers and she was powerless to do anything other than return his kiss. His sweet exploration left her scrambling to keep up but somehow managing to follow along.

Her nipples beaded as they scraped against his chiseled chest. The only thing standing between them was the lace of her cami, and Francy prayed that Dante didn't notice what was happening. She never knew when to take him seriously, and if this was another one of his bizarre proclamations or gestures, then she didn't want him to know that it meant so much more to her than to him.

The idea of humiliating herself by admitting to being in love with him was too much. He ran so hot-cold. One minute seeming to want her as badly as she did him and the next casting her out of his life—his very long life.

*This isn't right. You have someone else.*

Placing her palms on his chest, Francy pushed gently, needing to end his game before it got out of hand and she ended up begging him to make love to her. One round of begging like a pathetic puppy was more than enough for her. She'd never do that again. No. She was tougher than she'd been all those years ago. She was a different person. One who didn't require Dante to survive. Right?

Dante groaned and made a move to kiss her again. Francy shook her head as she laughed, knowing that if she bothered to try anything else, she'd only end up in tears. "Oh, you are good, buddy, but that will be enough of that."

"But . . ."

"Oh, but nothing. I think we, or rather, you, laid out the groundwork for our friendship very clearly for me. I listened and learned. Did you?"

Dante sighed, the remorse on his face was evident but she couldn't let him change the rules to suit himself. Not now. Not when so much was at stake for her. "Francy, it was different then."

"Different how? I'm still the same person I was when you explained that . . . oh . . . never mind. I didn't drive all this way to pick the scabs off old wounds. I came to see you before I have to leave. So what are we doing for the weekend? I thought we could drive into town so I can see how much, if any, it's changed. Oh, we need to go over to the cottage. I'd love to see what you've done with it. I still can't believe you took it on. It's not like you don't already have enough to worry about."

His brow furrowed and Francy had to fight the urge to smooth the crease away. "Leave? Aren't you moving home? You're finished with school now. I assumed you'd move back here. That was the plan. That's what we decided on, right?" The concern in his voice moved her.

She wanted to lie and tell him everything would be all right, but she wouldn't do that to Dante. Withholding the truth about her love for him for so many years had been painful enough. Flat out lying would destroy her. "I'm here now. Let's enjoy ourselves. We can spend the weekend together before I need to head back."

"The weekend?" Dante pulled her to him. The feel of his hard body pressed to her was almost too much. "Why just the weekend?" It was easy to see the wheels of thought spinning in his head. He'd always had eyes that seemed to bare his soul.

Now, as she stared into them, she fought with all she had to stay strong. Francy's insides clenched. For some reason she'd thought they'd have time to just be around each other before she had to drop the bomb on him. In her mind, they'd spend the weekend visiting places they used to frequent, talk a bit about their mutual friends and then she'd ease into the news she knew he'd hate. Obviously, that wasn't going to happen. "Dante."

He closed his eyes a moment and swallowed so hard that the cords moved in his thick neck, making her want to lick it. The idea was wrong for so many reasons but felt like it should be so right.

"What's going on? What are you not telling me?"

She sighed. He knew her well. Drawing in a deep breath, she prepared for the inevitable. "We need to talk."

Dante gathered her hands in his and gasped. "What the . . . ?"

"Dante, I didn't know how to tell you on the phone. It's why I came. I needed to tell you face-to-face." Francy let him lift her left hand higher and had to look away as he ran his finger over the engagement ring she now wore.

"Francy, no."

She choked back a sob. "I'm sorry. I wanted to tell you so many times. I just couldn't find the right words. I . . . I can't explain it, Dante."

"How long have you been with him?" he asked, his voice strained.

She focused on the Spanish-tile floor, anything to keep her mind and gaze off him. She knew how much she'd let him down, how much she'd hurt him, and it killed her. It would only hurt him more to find out that Ivon, the man she would be marrying, was a vampire. Not only that, but Ivon was as old as, if not older than, Dante. Nothing she had to tell Dante would please him. Still, it needed to be said. "I met him the day after I left for college."

"The day after I sent you away?" The hurt in his voice was evident.

Francy nodded, her throat feeling very dry all of the sudden. "Yeah."

"And not once in five years did you feel the need to share the fact that you were with someone? We talk on the phone at least once a month. You never thought once, in all that time, to let me in on this?"

Snorting, she cast him a wary glance. "Oh, like you shared details of your sex life with me."

Something passed over Dante's handsome face that she couldn't read and her instincts told her not to dwell on it. He lifted her hand even higher and plucked the ring from her finger.

"Dante!" She tried to grab it back but he held it high in the air. "Give it back."

"No. While you're here with me, you're *not* engaged."

"What?" she asked, going to her tiptoes in an attempt to retrieve the ring. "It doesn't work that way. Stop acting like a two-year-old. I should have told you sooner but this is ridiculous."

"*Aspetta un attimo!*"

Francy stared at him with a blank expression, unsure what he'd just said. Taking a deep breath, Dante appeared to get a handle on his emotions. That was a good thing. Francy was well aware of the beast he carried within him. Having him calm himself, even slightly, was imperative. The last thing she wanted was to be forced to use her powers against Dante. Not only could it harm him, it would emotionally kill her.

"Wait a minute! I am not the one who is acting like a child. I am not the one who stayed away so long. I have been here." He gave her a hard look. "I've said I was sorry for snapping at you, Francy. Emotions ran high that night. It wasn't something we planned or expected. I'd change it if I could. You didn't need to lash back like this. You could have just yelled at me. Telling me you're engaged seems a bit much."

"And said what?" She stopped trying to get the ring back and started shoving him as hard as she could. The only problem was he didn't budge. That didn't really surprise her. Dante was special, like her. Different from humans yet not like the monsters, the demons, they'd been born to fight. They were supernaturals sworn to uphold good. Sworn to protect unsuspecting humans from things that they thought existed only in their nightmares. It was who they were and who they would always be. "Why are we even having this conversation? It's not like we're anything more than friends."

"Oh, we are a hell of a lot more than that," he said, picking her up quickly.

She yelped and clung to him. His earthy smell moved over her, exciting her in ways it shouldn't. "What are you doing?"

Dante didn't answer. Instead, he backed her up against the wall and took her mouth with his. There was little time to protest. Dante had her skirt up around her hips and his hands on the backs of her thighs before she could blink. The knowledge that she didn't want to protest took her by surprise.

"Dante."

He cupped her ass cheeks and ground his hips against her. "I want you, Francy. Tell me that you don't want me. Tell me and I'll stop."

Her mind raced. The idea of him stopping, of his pelvis no longer grinding against hers, terrified her. Moaning, she held tight to Dante. "Please."

"Please what?"

"Please fuck me."

Sliding a finger under her thong, he sent shivers through her entire body as he skimmed across her swollen clit. It took everything in her not to cry out his name again. She clung to him, savoring the feel of his powerful frame.

DANTE GUERRASIO INCHED HIS TONGUE along Francy's outer ear, no longer bothering to control his breathing. He had more pressing issues, like the beast within him trying to surface, fighting to be free and finish what it had started to do five years earlier—claim its rightful mate.

How could she even presume to be engaged to another? She was his. His love. His everything. It didn't make any sense. She shouldn't have been able to love another. She was his true mate. That didn't come with light stipulations. That meant they were made for each other and no one else could come between them. Yet somehow, someone had managed to do just that.

Caressing Francy's swollen clit, he took in her floral scent as well as that of her arousal. Oh, she wanted him. That was easy to tell by her elevated heart rate, ragged breaths and soaked pussy.

How could she have even thought to try to replace him? Better yet, why had he felt the need to give her freedom to live away from him? Why had her need to see more, live away, learn about herself, been so important to him? He'd practically driven her off by forcing her to experience life on her own for a bit. Never did he suspect she'd take that as a sign he was shutting her out of his life.

All Dante had wanted was for his mate to never look back, never regret a moment they would spend together once he took her. He'd watched his mother struggle with "what ifs" his entire life and had vowed to never let his mate go through that. The only problem was that she had found someone else to quench the thirst he'd unlocked on the table in this very room five years ago.

Now she would see what he held back from her then. What he hadn't wanted to use to tie her to him before she was ready. She'd see him in full mating glory, his cock untiring and insatiable. It was what happened to his line of werewolves when the time came to claim their mates. He'd fuck her tight little cunt until she begged him never to allow another man to touch her.

"Please."

Her plea was soft, and Dante knew he couldn't answer it as gently as he wanted to. The beast within him demanded he take her and soon. Francy would either love it or hate him forever. With what he'd found on her finger only moments earlier, he knew he didn't have a choice. It had to be done.

Inserting a finger into her hot pussy, Dante growled out at the sensation. It was just as he remembered, tight, wet and welcoming. Too tight to have been well serviced by the man she'd dared to pledge her life to. The man he would hunt and kill. The very thought of Francy sharing herself with another set his inner beast on edge. The only thing that grounded him was the feel of having Francy back in his arms.

He could still remember the way her channel had held his fingers tightly as he drank her sweet cream. The very scent of it seemed to coat his tongue, reminding him of what he'd gone without for so long. He'd been unable and unwilling to take another to his bed after he pushed her to go. The very thought of sinking his cock into anyone that wasn't Francy turned his stomach. His mate was all he wanted.

For five years he lay in bed at night, fisting his cock as he pumped it to images, memories of Francy spread out on the table before him. The idea of her taking him in her mouth, her pussy, her ass, had kept him going. And with each release he would vow that one day soon he'd expel his seed in her, fill her with his child, his love, and start the family the gods always promised.

He held back, always wanting to go to her but afraid that he'd drag her home before she was ready. Now, as he thought about the situation, Dante realized that he should have gone to her. Should have laid claim to her, made her his long ago. He'd been a fool. A silly romantic who believed that love would indeed lead her back to him, not into the arms of another.

Unable to wait any longer, Dante freed his aching cock from the confines of his drawstring pants. It bobbed obscenely and he took hold of it, blindly seeking the entrance to Francy's wet core. Letting a claw extend from his fingertip, he cut the tiny string of her thong with ease, removing the only restriction that stood between him and paradise.

It was at this point last time that Francy's magik had broken loose and burned up the hearth. This time he was prepared. Slapping his dick against her clit, he encouraged added blood flow while grinning with the knowledge that he'd already made the beauty in his arms come so hard that she mystically started a fire. And that had been without even getting to sink his shaft into her.

As he pressed the head of his cock to her, she whimpered slightly in his ear. "Dante, a condom."

The very idea of covering himself, dulling the feeling of his mate's body accepting his was absurd. Each knew the other was supernatural, immune to human diseases. As far as pregnancy went, it was a matter that was left up to the gods. They determined when it was time for a mated couple to reproduce. Sure, they listened to prayers, dreams of the size of the family one wished to have, but in the end it was in their hands. If they deemed that he and Francy were to be blessed with a baby, then it would be, and he knew she wanted children. She always had. It was why he'd refused to fully claim her when he'd first been given the chance.

With as much as Francy desired to be a mother and as much as he wished to see her swollen with his child, Dante knew the gods would have answered them and that Francy never would have experienced life on her own. Never known what else was out there. But now she was ready to sign her life over to another—a man that wasn't her mate and who could never give her the family she had always wanted. It was time to take action. It was time to take Francy.

Easing the head of his cock into her slowly, he bit down hard on his lower lip in an attempt to keep from coming. "Francy . . . you're so fucking tight," he whispered, unsure how he was going to move another inch without finishing too soon. "You feel so good. Do you like that, baby? Do you like me entering you?"

"Dante, we need . . ."

"You need to let me finish what I started, Francy. Let me finish making you my wife. I started five years ago but didn't have the heart to complete the claiming until you'd had a chance to have a life of your own. Let me complete it now. Let me make you mine forever."

"What?"

"You are my true mate, Francy. Five years ago, in this very room, I began the claiming ritual. It's past time I finished it. Let me be in you. All of me. Nothing between us."

The confused look in her eyes answered the long-standing question he'd always had. He'd wondered if she knew what he had begun. It was clear that she had no idea that he, in the eyes of the supernatural world, had bound her to him with the promise of marriage. He should have known. It wasn't as though her family were shifters. Francy came from witches, not lycans. It was different for them. They didn't practice the same custom.

That night five years ago, he had proposed by starting the mating process and she had accepted his advances, rendering any proposals to come after him void. Fate gave Francy to him, and the nature of their supernatural species assured that they would be one. When he'd taken her, his mate, and begun to make love to her it was set in motion. He had started the claiming rights. With any other woman it wouldn't have mattered, but with Francy it did. She was his chosen one.

"Dante?" The question in her voice warmed his heart. There was no malice in her, only genuine concern. "I didn't know. I thought you didn't want me like that. That you only wanted me as a friend. I didn't know it was the start of a claiming."

"Is that a yes?"

"Yes," she whispered.

Surging forward, Dante buried himself to the hilt in her, crying out as he did. It was truly heaven within the walls of her body. He stilled, allowing her time to adjust to his size. "I do want you as my friend, Francy. My friend, my lover, my life mate, my wife and the mother of my children. I want it all and it's past time I took it."

Francy held tight to him and began to wiggle her hips ever so slightly. Long strands of auburn hair fell forward, covering half of her flawless face. As she stared up at him, one vivid blue eye visible beneath the veil of hair, he felt his heart melting. The fiery vixen had won his love upon first sight so many years ago and had only increased her hold on his soul as time wore on. Being in her, knowing he was stretching the lips of her pussy taut and she was loving every second, was more than he could handle.

Thrusting in and out of her, Dante lifted her higher so he could drive her down onto his throbbing cock. Francy cried out and bit down hard on his shoulder, causing the beast within him to answer her call. It moved through him quickly, lengthening his incisors and forcing him to lean forward. Before he could even think of stopping himself, he was piercing her skin, much the same way his dick was piercing her body, long and deep.

The coppery sweet taste of Francy's blood ran through him, invigorating him. He moved faster, pumping himself into his mate as he let her blood slide down his throat. The animal noises that sounded around them came from him but he didn't care. The need to be sure she was forever his was too great to be concerned about anything else.

He felt it then, her magik rising up to envelop him. Pressing to her firmly, Dante took extra care to assure that his lower abdomen rubbed against her clit as he resumed his piston-like thrusts. The animal in him wanted to drag her to the ground, unload his seed and then flip her over and fuck that tempting ass of hers. He struggled hard to maintain control.

As it stood, the feel of her cunt wrapped around his shaft was pushing the beast toward the winning point. Dante fought to stay in control but Francy made it difficult, moaning, running her hands over his body while she kissed him passionately.

"Dante, please." Francy's velvet voice ran over him, causing his stomach muscles to tighten, indicating an orgasm fast approaching. "There, Dante. There. Gods yes, fuck me harder. There. Mmm. So close."

The second her pussy began grasping him, pulling him back into its oasis, Dante knew Francy was coming. Her sweet cunt fisted him and he wanted to howl out in victory. He didn't. Instead, he held tight to her as his balls drew up and his cock began to jet seed into her.

"*Amore,*" he whispered, licking the wound on her neck closed as the last of his semen filled her. It was done. She was officially his wife now and nothing could ever change that. There would be no more five-year spans between tasting her lips and holding her in his arms.

# TWO

FRANCY WIGGLED ON THE KING-SIZED BED, a bit restless as she waited for Dante to return from the hunt. He'd left shortly after their lovemaking session in the kitchen and had not returned. The sun had already set for the day, and Francy was doing her best to remain calm. The wolf he carried within had sensed something dangerous in the surrounding area and had left Dante little chance of ignoring it. Not that Dante ever would. He took his destiny seriously and let no evildoer go unpunished. He was a protector—the product of a witch and a werewolf.

He hailed from Italy and had been here for many decades before she'd even been born. Dante had entered into her life when she was fifteen, around the same time that she came into her powers. When her father had taken her before the council, as was standard with all of-age witches, they put forth a call on her behalf. It wasn't until five years ago, near the hearth downstairs, that she'd learned that Dante was the one they had summoned. Now she knew why. He was her mate.

*Ivon.*

The very thought of the man she'd promised to marry, the

man who waited for her now back in the city, sickened her. Francy's intent when coming to visit Dante had truly been honorable. She'd never wanted to hurt Ivon. It was hard enough to know that the mere mention of coming to the countryside had upset Ivon—his finding out she'd mated with another man would be the lowest blow yet. As much as Dante disliked her being around vampires, Ivon disliked lycans. It wasn't as though this was common. Other vampires and lycans had no problems getting along.

*I won't be helping their opinions on the matter any.*

No part of her had thought that she'd fall into Dante's arms. He'd seemed so headfast, so sure that she needed to move away from him, that she'd assumed he didn't desire her as she did him.

It was obvious she'd been wrong. So wrong in fact that she'd betrayed another. A man she still couldn't understand her attraction to but had promised her hand to all the same.

*How the hell am I going to break this to Ivon? He'll want to come and try to work it out. I'm sure of it. Dante won't stand for that.*

Francy's chest tightened as her mind raced. This was all too much. Too soon. A whirlwind that she couldn't seem to find her footing in, nor did she have any desire to change what had happened.

It was wrong and she knew it. She also knew that she loved Dante with all of her heart. What she had with Ivon, while wonderful, was so very different. For some reason, Francy felt removed from it all. It made sense when she was with him. But once she stepped away and looked at the situation, she wondered why she'd ever agreed to marry him to begin with.

*I love Dante.* The proclamation chased some of the guilt away and left her thinking of her mate. Running a hand over her lower stomach, Francy closed her eyes and wished with all of her heart that she now carried his child. If the gods offered their blessing, then she and Dante could very well be parents before the year was out. It was something she had always dreamed of, and when Dante had carried her up the stairs, she'd found herself slipping into his mind, reading his thoughts. It was a trick they would perfect over time. All mates could do it. It had taken her by surprise at first and when she found him hoping that their union would produce a large family she couldn't help but smile.

Francy slid her hand down further, running her fingers through the juicy aftermath of their lovemaking, skimming over her clit in the process. Fire shot through her inner thighs as she made another pass by her swollen bud. Biting her lip, she did her best to keep from crying out in agony as her body burned with desire. *I need you, Dante.*

*Amore.* Dante used their bonded link for the first time to communicate with her.

"Yes?" she said, out loud, not yet comfortable with the idea of speaking with her mind. Dante seemed to hear her as if she'd pushed with her mind, so Francy went with it.

*I can see you in my mind, spread out on the bed, touching yourself, and I know that you're thinking about me. I know that you want me there, licking you, fucking you, coming in you. Show me how right I am.*

That drove her onward. Francy opened her legs more and began methodically rubbing her clit, wishing it was Dante's tongue there. She could almost feel his sexual frustration even with the distance between them. "Are you safe?"

*I was until I was suddenly hit with images of my wife pleasuring herself.*

*Now I'm in danger of my own needs killing me. Every ounce of me wants to have my cock buried deep within you, wants to experience this with you.* She sensed his sigh. *I can smell your sweet cunt, Francy, and I want to be there tasting it.*

"I want you here tasting it too," she whispered. It was the truth. All she'd ever wanted was Dante. Knowing that he was now, in the eyes of the supernatural community, her husband, her mate for eternity, only served to increase her need to find sexual release.

*Come for me. I want to see you touching yourself as you think of me while I continue to hunt whatever it is that's out here.*

"Is that safe?"

He chuckled. *It's a hell of a lot safer than depriving me of what I want. Don't think I'll go easy on you if I have to return with a dick so hard it could impale you. I'll fuck that sweet ass of yours, Francy. I'll bend you over and mount you. Mmm, I'm hard just thinking about it—about you.*

"Mmm." She let out a soft laugh. "I don't know, Dante. I'd rather have you here touching me."

*Do it, Francy. I need it. Let me experience you masturbating. Let me watch and feel it through our otherworldly bond.*

Giving in, Francy rubbed faster and lowered her other hand. She inserted a finger into her wet channel and continued to stimulate herself. The very thought of Dante's body entering hers pushed her close to her zenith.

"I can't. Not without you." No sooner did the words leave her mouth then she felt something warm draw her clit upward. Gasping, Francy opened her eyes to find Dante leaning down, licking and sucking on her. It was one of the most erotic sights she'd ever seen. "Dante."

He moaned, the sound vibrating through her pussy as he stared up at her with dark, haunted eyes. The passion and lust in them shook her to her very core. All those years of believing that he'd turned her away, wanting only to be friends, had been wasted. Dante was the man she was born for and she had denied him for too long.

He swirled his tongue over her clit and she writhed beneath his expert touch. Clutching the sheets, Francy tipped her head back and let the pleasure of her orgasm wash over her. Dante slid his long tongue into her, lapping up her cream, prolonging her pleasure.

"No more," she pleaded, unable to take another single second of the mind-numbing sensations moving throughout her body.

Dante ignored her as his gaze bore through her and his tongue continued to work its magik, forcing her to peak again and again. She lay there, so wet, so stimulated that she bordered on numbness. When Dante slid his finger into her ass she jolted, the intrusion surprising, and he chuckled into her pussy.

The strange fullness that followed as he finger-fucked her ass did nothing in the way of stopping the seemingly endless on-slaught of pleasure. It built slowly at first as her body grew accustomed to the bizarre feeling of fullness. Dante added another finger and she immediately drew in a sharp breath.

"Relax and push down, *amore*." Dante licked her clit, easing her fears and allowing her to loosen a bit. "Has anyone ever taken you here, Francy?" His voice was suddenly cold and his gaze hard. "Did *he* take you here?"

"No," she said, panting. Until now, the very idea of a man fucking her ass had never occurred to her. Having Dante's finger in her, she knew that she wouldn't be completely satisfied until she was permitted the pleasure of his cock in her ass as well.

"How could you let another man touch you? Pleasure you? Love you, Francy?"

No part of her wanted this conversation to take place period, let alone in the middle of what they were sharing. Reaching down, she cupped the sides of his face and tipped her head. "I didn't know, honey. I swear it's true."

It was easy to see that he understood that fact when he nodded ever so slightly, but it didn't erase the hurt on his face. Francy let her magik build before running it over Dante's lower lip with the pad of her thumb. "I love you."

His gaze snapped to her face. For a moment, he looked confused and then shocked. How he could be surprised by her admission was beyond her. She'd been in love with him from the day she met him but their age difference prevented either of them from acting upon it.

"Francy?"

"This is where you tell me that you love me too, Dante."

With his supernatural speed, he moved up and over her quickly, hooking an arm under her right leg and lifting it as he entered her. His cock filled her, spreading the walls of her channel to the brink of tearing. Thankfully, he'd more than prepared her. Her wet pussy still managed to grip his shaft, demanding that he stay rooted in her.

"*Ti amo*—I love you." As the words fell from his lips Francy felt her very soul, her essence, reaching out to meet his. The beast and the man answered her mystical search, merging with her on all planes of existence, binding them even more than the claiming had.

Dante's lips captured hers as their merged magik set out, caressing them in places they never dreamed could be reached and leaving them both so close to coming that they shared a moan a second before they shared an orgasm. His hot seed filled her quickly. Being connected to him caused Francy to experience what he did. She knew how her pussy felt around his thick, long cock and she knew how good he felt in her.

His jaw dropped and his eyes swirled with flecks of solid black as a growl tore free of him. Dante moved his hands away from her, leaving the entire weight of his body pressed to her. Riding out her orgasm, she tipped her head and found that his hands had shifted. Long claws and the starts of honey-colored fur hovered above the bed.

Her heart sped as she considered screaming and bucking him off her. Dante growled again. "Don't, Francy. Don't be scared, it makes it harder for me to control the beast. I can smell your fear and it makes me want to pin you to the floor, mount you and fuck that sweet ass until sunrise."

"Dante?" she asked, unable to push her fears away.

He shook his head slightly, his jaw tight and the cords in his neck popping out. "Please, Francy. Don't be scared. I would never hurt you. I love you."

Before she could respond, something pinched deep within her lower abdomen. Drawing in a ragged breath, Francy's eyes widened. "Dante, something's wrong." A strange fuzzy feeling washed over her. It held a magik she didn't recognize and it seemed fixated on her womb.

Dante took a deep breath and a feral smile spread over his face. "You accepted my seed, Francy. The gods blessed us."

"The gods blessed . . . ?" It hit her then. Tears welled quickly in the corners of her eyes as she reached out and brought his clawed hands to the sides of her face. Any fear she had of Dante fled and she planted tiny kisses in his palms. "We're pregnant?"

"Yes, *amore*, we are." His hands shifted back into human form while she held them. Dante stroked her cheeks, wiping away her tears. When his lips found hers, she surrendered herself to his kiss, knowing that he was every bit as happy as she was.

FRANCY PICKED A HANDFUL OF STRAWBERRIES and placed them in her basket before moving forward to the next bed. Dante's gardens were extensive and spanned the western side of his home. The smell of rosemary, oregano and thyme filled the air around her, invigorating her. She'd awoken hungry and feeling a bit worn. That was to be expected after having spent the night in the arms of her insatiable husband. With the dawn several hours out, she was hoping to be able to surprise Dante with breakfast when he woke.

At random times she'd woken to find Dante slipping his cock into her. His excuse had been that he was making up for lost time. In truth, he needed no excuse. She had no problem allowing him to find pleasure in her because she found pleasure with him as well.

Smoothing down the pale green ankle-length skirt she wore, Francy couldn't help but smile as she thought about Dante hiding her undergarments from her. After they showered together, she'd gone to put some on only to find him grinning mischievously.

After twenty minutes of searching his mansion she gave up and slept next to him naked.

Francy ran her hand over her bare midriff, trying to imagine what her stomach would look like in several months. As she stared down at the cropped white vest that she wore, she knew it would be a thing of the past very soon. Already, it barely contained her breasts, coming just shy of showing her nipples to the world.

Something rustled in the trees surrounding the gardens, catching her attention and leaving an odd sensation prickling over her skin. The hair on the back of her neck rose and her gut told her to get back to the house. Back to Dante. There was still an hour before sunrise and she knew better than to wander to the edges of the property, but the lure of making him breakfast had been too great to pass up.

Turning to rush back to the house, Francy found herself standing face-to-face with the one person she never dreamed to run into at Dante's—her now ex-fiancé.

"Ivon?"

"Surprise," he said, his French accent thick. That was never a good thing. It usually meant that he was upset about something. "I thought you might be lonely, coming up to stay at your parents' cottage all by yourself, so I decided to join you."

Francy watched him closely. Something was very off with him. His normally blue eyes were as dark as the sky surrounding them, and his ear-length chestnut brown hair was disheveled. Ivon was normally one who appeared together at all times. This was different.

Ivon glanced back toward Dante's house and nodded his head. "Hmm, it is so much bigger than you described it, Francy."

"That's because it's not my parents' cottage. The cottage is down that trail that leads through the woods," she said, knowing that she had to tell him the truth. She'd mated with another man and was now Dante's wife. Not to mention that she was pregnant with his child.

"You are a long way from it, Francy." Ivon took a step toward her. His all-black ensemble added to the menacing air about him. He'd never intimidated her before. Why now? "Care to tell me why you're on Dante Guerrasio's property and why you wear his scent?"

"You know Dante?"

The smile that covered Ivon's face scared her. "Oh, he and I go way back. I am surprised that he has not told you all about his first love."

Francy drew in a sharp breath. First love? Ivon moved toward her with a speed he shouldn't possess, even for someone with his powers. He was standing before her in the blink of an eye. He caressed her cheek with the back of his hand. "Did he forget to mention that to you before he fucked you? That is what he did, is it not? Did he fuck you, Francy?"

She tried to back up but Ivon slid his hand behind her and cupped her neck. "Ivon . . ."

"Answer me, Francy. Did he fuck you?" He tipped his head down, centering his gaze on her. "Did you open yourself to him, knowing you told me that you would spend eternity with me?"

"You don't understand. Dante had already started the mating process before I met you." She pleaded with her eyes. "I didn't know."

"Mating process?" Ivon's eyes narrowed. "Are you telling me

that you are his true mate?" A sick-looking smile crept over him slowly, making Francy's stomach clench.

She didn't answer. It turned out she didn't have to. Ivon laughed, and the sound made her skin crawl and confused her even more. "Ah, this is so fitting. He had an affair with my true mate, leaving me no choice but to kill her to avoid the shame it would bring me to claim her, and now I have spent five years paying him back—fucking his true mate, making her scream out my name and beg me for more."

"Get away from her," Dante said, his voice hard.

Francy tried to look behind her to see Dante but Ivon refused to ease his hold on her neck. He glanced over her shoulder and seemed to take great pride in the situation. "I came expecting to find Francy fucking some ex-lover, a human even. Never in my wildest dreams did I suspect she would be fucking you." He licked his lower lip. "Tell me, Dante. Did you ever dream that it was me she has been fucking for five years? That it was me that she agreed to wed?"

Dante growled, the sound so loud that it vibrated through Francy. Ivon made a move to go at Dante but Francy put her hands up quickly and pressed them to his chest. "I need to talk to you, Ivon." She glanced at the ground. "I can't . . ."

"You wish to tell me what I have already figured out, Francy." He reached down and cupped her sex, taking her by surprise. "You let him cram his dick in you. You let him fill you full of his animal seed and you let him mark you as his."

"Ivon, what in the hell is wrong with you?" she asked, doing her best to understand his complete personality turnaround. "This doesn't sound like you. Where's the man who spent countless nights making me laugh as he spun me around our kitchen to old swing music? Where's the man who whispered sweet nothings in French every chance he got?"

A low jealous growl emanated from Dante. Guilt consumed her as she glanced at her mate.

"The second you gave yourself to that animal, you killed that part of me, Francy." He pulled her to him and stared down at her. "Denounce his claim on you and come home with me now. I swear to you that I will make his death quick and painless if you do."

Death? Quick and painless?

Francy fought down the sick feeling in her stomach and shook her head. "Ivon, you can't hurt Dante. It was his right to finish the mating ritual. And he couldn't have done it if I didn't want it to happen. I didn't plan on it, on him, but I can tell you that I refuse to regret it or wish it away." She stood tall, not wanting to show how very afraid of him she now was. "I'm sorry that I hurt you. That was never my intent."

Ivon laughed. "Please, Francy. Do not tell me that you believe his bedroom lies. He promised Edeline the world, his eternal love and protection. He followed through on none of those."

"Edeline?" she asked, doing her best to keep up with it all.

Ivon traced the outline of her nipple while he pressed his mouth to her ear, and she shuddered with disgust. "She was to be my mate until she allowed that filthy beast to enter her. Tell me, how does it make you feel knowing that he loved someone before you came along? That he wanted to spend his life with her?"

As hard as Francy tried to fight it, her jealous streak kicked in to full gear.

*He lies, Francy,* Dante's voice boomed through her head. *She came to me, scared of him, seeking refuge. I offered her that but nothing more. I swear to you. It was never sexual between us, Francy. Never. You are the only woman I've loved, Francy. You know that's true.*

She rolled her eyes. *Ivon may not be acting like himself at the moment, but he would never lie to me.*

*Really? Then did he tell you that he's one of the heads of the Dark Council?*

The Dark Council was evil through and through. Thoughts of her five years with Ivon flooded her mind. All the nights that he had to leave on sudden business trips, all the times that he would call and cancel plans, all the times he'd hold her close as if hiding her when around his friends—it all made sense. Had he used black magik on her to make her want him? Was that why she'd felt the odd pull to him?

Before Francy could question Ivon about it, he was dipping his head down and sniffing her stomach. He hissed, flashing fang as he went. "You carry the animal's child."

He seized hold of her quickly, lifted her off her feet and glared at her through fully shifted vampire eyes. "Edeline, how dare you do this to me? You know who I am. You know my position on the council, yet you seek to embarrass me by running to that . . . that *thing* for help. Why? Because you could not handle the truth about me?"

What? Ivon had gone mad. She wasn't Edeline.

"I'm not . . . Ivon, please."

He sneered. "Beg for your life and that of the child you now carry. I want to hear it passing over your lips as I teach you once and for all that if you do not belong to me, then you belong to no one."

"Ivon." Francy clutched on to his arm in an attempt to ease the pressure on her throat. "You're hurting me—Francy, not Edeline."

Ivon laughed deeply. "Can you not sense her around you, Francy? It is what first drew me to you. She is your guide, your protector from the other side—a gift from the gods. I should have known that he was your mate. Edeline would tell me again and again how sorry she felt for him, not having a true mate, not knowing real love. I should have known that she was standing by your side, protecting you, guiding you to him. Her heart literally bled for him in the end. As will yours."

Francy clutched tighter to his arm as she stared into his hate-filled eyes. "Ivon, don't do this. I can feel your pain. You're letting the demon within you make decisions for you." A breeze kicked up from out of nowhere. It surrounded her, lifting her hair and whispering without words. The sudden knowledge of who it was, Edeline, and what she was saying hit her. She gasped and agreed to what Edeline wanted. Closing her eyes, Francy allowed the presence to enter her.

When she opened her mouth to speak, it wasn't her voice that came out. "Ivon."

He stilled, no doubt shocked by the sound of Edeline's voice.

"You misdirect your rage. It was not you that I ran from, scared for my life and that of our child. It was the demon you carry within you."

Ivon's brow furrowed, his dark gaze seeming to search Francy for answers she could only pray she had. "Edeline? A child?"

"*Oui.*"

"How are you here?"

"I watch over her, Ivon. You said it yourself, I am her spirit guide. But I am more than that to her. It was I who went to the gods upon my death, choosing not to seek vengeance on you but to repay another man's kindness." Francy felt her hand lifting as she pointed back at Dante but knew that it wasn't she who controlled the action. "Dante did nothing other than act as an ear for my concerns about you. He agreed to help me try to reach you through the demon that had taken control."

Ivon snarled, his face twisting as it partially shifted into its vampire form. "You lie."

"Ivon, you feel the truth of my words. Dante was your best friend. He only wanted to help you find your way back to me— to our child. To try to pin my murder upon him was beyond a betrayal. Had the High Council not discovered you were working for the Dark Council, Dante would have been executed."

"They should have killed him."

"No." The force within Francy did its best to soothe her as it revealed things she did not know. "He deserved to live, to be happy. You know this is true, Ivon. Look deep within and you will find the answer there."

Ivon rolled his eyes, still seeming confused by it all.

"That is why I went to the gods, Ivon. I told them every tiny detail that I had ever heard Dante reveal to you about what he wanted in his mate. Each time you would talk with him, pry information about what he wanted in a woman, I listened. And I remembered."

An odd feeling of peace, of absolute happiness, surged through Francy and she knew that the spirit that spoke through her was proud of her decision to go to the gods. "I told them and they listened with open minds and hearts. Once they deemed the threat you posed to his future mate was long past, they created her. They sent her spirit forth to be born unto this Earth. She was created for him, made to be everything he had ever wanted and so very much more. It is something the gods hold sacred, Ivon. Something they insisted I help guard. I was sent the day she came into her powers to watch over her, to keep her from being harmed by you or any like you."

The wicked laugh that came from Ivon made Francy shiver. Edeline didn't seem fazed by it. "I know the thoughts that now run through your head, Ivon. You think that Dante's mate did not love him enough to resist you. That is not true. I did not know that I was able to push my will on her or that Francy was sensitive enough to respond to it. When I saw you, I could not stop my-self. I went to you. It was natural for her to follow. It was my need to see the goodness in you once again that blinded her to everything—that gave you access to her bed. Not her own. She has loved only one man and she now calls him her husband."

"No." Shock was evident on Ivon's face. As much as Francy feared him, she also felt fear for him. If he couldn't fight his demon for the woman he truly loved—Edeline—then he had lit-tle hope of being reached now. She wanted him to fight it, to push his demon down, but she wanted her child's safety more.

"Ivon, did you know that she called Dante every free moment she had? Did you know that her heart hurt the day you asked for her hand, and I was so taken with your kindness and warmth that I pushed her to say yes? She spent the next day in tears, knowing that her heart belonged to another but too confused to realize what was happening."

The shock of it all hit Francy as she listened to the truth come forth from her own mouth. "She has always been and will only ever be in love with one man and he is restraining himself as we speak to afford me this chance at redeeming you. He does this because at one point you were his best friend, but know that he will not allow harm to come to Francy. She is his wife, the mother of his child and the only one his heart has ever belonged to. She is our gift to him, Ivon—our thank-you for trying to fix us."

Ivon thrust his power out, pushing Edeline's essence from Francy as he lifted her higher in the air. "If that is true, then she is a gift I no longer wish him to have."

Francy screamed out as pain shot through her. She wanted to fight back but it was all happening too fast. Something drew upon her power quickly, using it to strike out at Ivon. He dropped her and she fell to the ground.

*Stay down!*

The command came a second before Francy would have stood. She obeyed Dante, realizing he was the one who had drawn on her powers, and stayed low to the ground. In a flash he was leaping over her, his claws unsheathed. He struck out at Ivon. Francy watched as a cloud of dust encircled Dante. Everything looked like slow motion. Her breath caught. Ivon was dead.

Cool energy wrapped around her for a moment before Dante dropped to his knees. "Francy, are you hurt?"

Shaking mostly from the shock of it all, she cupped his cheek. "I'm sorry."

"Shh, it wasn't your fault. You loved me. You heard Edeline explain it. You didn't betray me or our bond." He held her tight, chasing away her inner demons. "It's okay, Francy. They're together again and we're together. No one's between us. No one's pushing the other to something they don't want. It's just us."

A tiny tickle of power ran through her lower abdomen, instantly calming her nerves. "Well, and baby makes three."

Dante's breath caught. "The baby's fine?"

"Yes." She took his hand in hers and ran it over her stomach. "He's fine."

"We'll have a boy?" he asked, smiling as he lifted her into his arms. "The first of many."

# EPILOGUE

*D*ANTE WOKE TO THE SWEET SENSATION of warm lips over his erect cock. As he took in the erotic sight of his wife filling her mouth with him, he slid his hands down into her long auburn locks and ground his teeth at the pleasure she was bringing him. The pleasure that she would forever bring him now that nothing stood between them. Edeline had given him a gift he could never thank her enough for. She'd given him his true love.

The tip of his dick hit the back of Francy's throat, yet she showed no signs of discomfort. Not even when her gag reflex kicked in, causing her mouth to water around his cock. She let out a sultry laugh as she sucked on him harder.

Francy seemed to need to taste him every bit as much as he needed her to do it. She hummed softly over him, sending him dangerously close to the edge of filling her mouth and throat with his cum.

"Francy." Holding her hair gently, he tried to ease her off him but she refused to move, opting for licking him as though he were a lollipop. Each swipe was pure torture—one he hoped he would be forced to endure for centuries.

Another throaty laugh escaped her. "Mmm, do you like that? You twitch whenever I do that."

Unable to think past the fact that she now had her teeth pressed to his tender flesh, scraping them against it, sending his body into a spasm, he simply nodded.

Francy laughed again. "How about this?" She slid a finger into her tempting mouth and pulled it out, slick and wet.

Dante watched with nothing short of rapture on his face as she tugged gently on his balls before easing her finger into his ass. Pleasure shot through him as she crooked it ever so slightly, pressing it to his prostate, filling him.

Quickly, she covered him with her mouth in time to catch the cum that shot forth from his convulsing cock. She kept her finger in his ass, fucking him slowly as he continued to come in jetting waves down her throat. Her purring only served to drive him onward, making him come even more than he normally would. "Enough."

Francy shook her head, looking every bit the siren she truly was. "It's not nearly enough, Dante."

He reached down and brought her up and over his still-hard cock. Part of him wondered if he'd ever be able to satisfy his need for Francy. Somehow, he knew he never would. She was his other half and he'd never tire of her.

As he lowered her body, allowing himself to spear her sweet pussy, he growled out. The feel of her already beginning to milk him before they'd even begun was almost too much. *"Amore,"* he whispered, nearly begging her to show him mercy.

Francy pressed her palms to his chest and sent a toe-curling surge of magik through his system. It felt as though hundreds of tiny mouths were kissing, sucking, his skin. When she leaned forward and captured his lips with hers he knew that she held a power over him that no one else ever would. He may have over a century on her but she had his heart, and in the end that was all that mattered.

He probed her mouth with his tongue and her pussy with his hungry cock. Thrusting his hips upward, Dante moaned as he felt her channel grasping hold of him. Immortal as he was, as they were, he knew she would be the death of him. Her love was toxic and it was one he'd gladly accept again and again.

Francy clawed his chest as she came with a start. Her pussy fisted his cock tightly and he gave in to the need to fill her again. She collapsed on him, her breathing shallow and her pulse speeding. "I love you, Dante."

"And I love you. *Solo tu*—only you, Francy."

The soft sounds of their son sleeping came over the baby monitor. He chuckled. "I love him as well, of course. As you would say, and baby makes three."

Kissing his collarbone, she purred slightly. "Honey, we need to change that to baby makes four."

"What?" Dante could hardly believe his ears. "The gods blessed us again?"

"Are you upset?"

"Upset that I have the woman I love in my arms, a healthy, happy son, another child on the way and an eternity with my family? No, Francy, I'm not upset. I am quite possibly the happiest man alive."

"So that means that you might be willing to do something spectacular with pasta for me?"

Dante couldn't help but pull her closer to him as he laughed. "Ah, craving again?"

"Mmm hmm." She nuzzled her lips to his neck and kissed him. "For pasta and you. You were more than worth the wait, Dante."

"As were you, *amore*."

# TEMPTED BY TWO

## ANYA BAST

# ONE

THEO WATCHED THE GLASS SLIP from Miranda's fingers and crash to the floor as the goblin walked into the restaurant.

"Oh, my God," she breathed.

He exchanged a quick glance with Miranda's best friend, Olivia. It was clear that Miranda could see the goblin and that only meant one thing.

She possessed fae blood.

For Theo, it explained everything. He understood then that, on some level, he'd already known Miranda had fae heritage. He simply hadn't realized it. From day one he'd felt a strong pull toward her. In fact, he'd never felt drawn to a woman this way, not this powerfully. Not even once in his very long life.

He should've realized it earlier.

Miranda stared with wide eyes at the greenish-colored creature in the doorway. Her blue-green eyes were like a sea, emotions ebbing and flowing within them. Theo clenched his fists in his lap, wanting nothing more than to comfort her. He wanted to reach over and tangle his fingers gently through her blonde curls, draw her close to him for comfort. But that would seem strange to her since Miranda didn't know about her heritage yet. She didn't feel the pull like he did. Not yet. She was attracted to him, Theo knew that much, but the attraction was shallow.

For the moment.

If he nurtured it, it would bloom.

"What's going on?" asked Will. He was one of Olivia's mates and was also a Gaelan warrior. Olivia's other mate, Mason, sat on her opposite side.

"The doorway," Olivia replied tersely. The goblin turned and fixed his gaze on the table. "There's a full-blood here who wants to see you and Mason."

Mason and Will both centered their gazes on the goblin, and then slid from their seats.

"Want me to come?" Olivia asked.

Mason shook his head and looked meaningfully at Miranda. "You better stay." Will and Mason walked toward the goblin. The three of them talked quietly, and then left the restaurant. They'd been working on a case for some time now and this was possibly related to it. Olivia was in training, learning how to wield her newfound abilities as a seer and find her place as third in a Gaelan partnership, but she wasn't ready yet to fully engage in Gaelan business.

Olivia exhaled slowly and examined the remnants of the Chinese food on the table. "That's either a break . . . or it's trouble."

Miranda stared blankly at the large fish tank behind Theo's chair. "Guys, I think I-I might be sick. Maybe I need to go home and sleep for a while. I'm seeing things."

Olivia covered Miranda's hand with her own. "You're not sick, sweetie. I saw it too."

Miranda's wide eyes snapped to her friend. "You saw that-that thing?"

"It was a goblin," said Theo, "a full-blooded adult goblin. A servant to a kingpin, most likely."

Realization swept over Miranda's face. She laughed. "This is some kind of practical joke! You hired that guy to come in here all dressed up, and you're acting like he's real."

"No, honey," Olivia answered. "We didn't—"

Miranda turned to the waitress who'd come to clean up the shattered glass. "Miss, did you see that man who just came in with that mask on?"

The waitress's brow furrowed. "Uhhh."

"He was wearing a blue shirt, tan pants and a black jacket."

"I saw a man dressed that way, miss, but he wasn't wearing a mask." She smiled. "Actually, he was pretty cute."

Miranda's face fell.

"It's glamour," Olivia said quickly in a whisper, letting the waitress finish cleaning up. "Goblins use a glamour, a type of magick, to disguise themselves as human. Only some people can see through the glamour. Hobgoblins, the smaller and less dangerous of the species are skilled with glamour. The full-blood goblins are less skilled, but they're the ones you really have to watch out for."

"Okay, I'll play along. If only some people can see through the glamour, why could *I* see through it?"

Theo glanced at Olivia. "You're a seer. You have something in your genetic makeup that gives you that ability. It's very rare.

Olivia has it too. The skill can come upon you at any time." He paused. "Now is apparently your time."

"What kind of *something?*" Miranda asked suspiciously.

Theo drew a breath. This was too much for her, too soon. "Fae blood, Miranda."

She laughed and clapped her hands with delight. "This is fun. You guys have great imaginations. So how is it my best friend just happens to have fae blood too?"

Theo paused for a moment in thought before speaking. "It's actually not that big a coincidence. On some level, you both sensed blood kinship and it drew you closer. In other words, subconsciously, like attracts like. You bonded as friends because on some level you knew you shared something."

If only she knew just how true that statement was. Theo had been attracted to Miranda in a deep way from the moment he'd first met her. It had been very strong, but he hadn't known until Miranda had seen the goblin that it was because she had fae blood. That fact, coupled with the unusual attraction he had to her, meant that she was his mate. Theo had no doubt of that. Not only was she his mate, she was Marco's mate as well.

Miranda was their third.

Theo sat staring into Miranda's blue-green eyes. Confusion bled into anger. She was meant to link with him and Marco. Happiness and fierce possessiveness surged through him.

"Okay, joke's over," Miranda replied. "You've gone far enough. It's really funny and all, but come clean. You guys are starting to piss me off."

Olivia looked uncomfortable. "It's no joke, Miranda. Plus . . . there's more, but you need to absorb this before you hear the rest.

We didn't have any idea that you would be able to see through glamour. I'm sorry we're not more prepared to explain things to you."

"I should have known," Theo said meaningfully. "I should've guessed."

Olivia's gaze snapped to his and held. Theo could tell she knew exactly what he wasn't saying out loud.

Miranda leaned forward and forced Theo's gaze to her face. "Look, I really like you, but I'm getting sick of this and you guys are scaring me half to death." She stood and grabbed her coat and purse. Before leaving, she leveled her gaze at Olivia. "And *you* just have no excuse."

Olivia and Theo watched Miranda leave. He wanted to follow, but Olivia was right, Miranda needed time to think about what had just happened.

"She's pissed," said Olivia mournfully.

"No, she's not pissed; she's scared."

Olivia nodded, then leaned forward, rested her head in her hands and groaned. "What the hell just happened? I thought Miranda was normal, human . . . one-hundred-percent *human*." She lifted her head and stared at him. "And you! You thought she might not be completely human and you didn't say anything?"

"I wasn't sure. I only suspected because I'm strongly attracted to her. Now I know it's not just lust."

"God, this is wild." Olivia shook her head. Her brown shoulder-length hair slid over her shoulders. "That was her first time. Poor Miranda."

"If the blood is there, the skill can awaken at any moment. She's lucky we were here. Otherwise she might have gone for months not knowing what was going on and afraid to tell any-one. She might've ended up like you, thinking she was crazy."

Olivia nodded. "You're right." She bit her lower lip. "What are you going to do?"

Something clenched hard and fast inside Theo as those words were spoken out loud. He felt elated and protective all of a sud-den. "I'm going to make her mine."

"Don't you mean *ours*? There's Marco to consider too."

A feeling of possessiveness made Theo grit his teeth. He had to admit there was something inside him that didn't want to share. He didn't answer her.

UNSEEN BY THE SHOPPERS AROUND HIM, Theo leaned back and watched Miranda. As a full-blooded Tylwyth Teg, he had the ability to use glamour to disguise himself. He wasn't quite invisi-ble in the formal sense of the word. He'd made himself unremark-able. When a person's gaze landed on him, he or she hardly noted his existence and then forgot him the moment they looked away.

Miranda allowed the salesperson to fasten the strap of the red high-heeled shoe around her ankle. Theo envied him. When the salesman—the *male* salesperson—smiled at her a little too long, masculine interest flickering over his face, Theo clenched his fists.

Theo wanted her, wanted her more than he'd ever wanted a woman. From the first time he'd seen her, the first time he'd scented her perfume, he'd wanted her. Now that he knew she was the third in his Gaelan partnership, he wanted her with a soul-deep hunger that nearly made him insane. The knowledge had triggered something primal inside him. After all, he had been waiting hundreds of years for her.

But he had to go slow. Miranda was being initiated into a world completely foreign to her. If he moved too fast, he'd only end up pushing her away.

He watched her walk across the floor to a mirror to admire the pretty shoes. The salesman watched her with appreciation in his eyes.

Theo wanted just a little time with her, watching her, when she was his alone, because he knew she wasn't. His partner, Marco, also had a claim on her, the same deep and inexorable claim that he had. Theo knew it was wrong to keep the knowledge of their third from Marco, but he just couldn't seem to help himself.

He just wanted one more day of her to himself. Of course, he'd said that yesterday and the day before that.

He *would* tell Marco soon.

Maybe tomorrow.

Miranda apparently had decided to buy the shoes. So Theo watched as she had the clerk box them up and she paid. He couldn't get the image of her in just the shoes and nothing else out of his mind. He could imagine her skin, soft peaches and cream, against the black comforter on his bed. The red shoes would look good against both his comforter and against her pale, pretty skin.

Her long legs would look good wrapped around his waist while he shafted long and hard into her.

Theo blew out a hard breath of frustration. He wanted her with everything he was. He wanted to keep her safe in the circle of his embrace, give her everything. Theo knew Marco would want the same—would want to cherish her, protect her, pamper her . . . love her.

As he followed her out of the store and down the mall to a bar, he thought about the ways he'd take her when he finally had her in his bed. He wanted to hear her whispers, her sighs and moans in his ear. He wanted her silky skin under his hands, while he was buried root-deep inside her eager pussy. The mere thought of it made him hard.

In the shadowy entranceway of the bar, Theo disengaged the concealment spell he'd cast on himself and entered a good ways behind her. It was crowded. She took a seat at the far end of the bar and he took one near the entrance.

A black haired man in his mid-thirties immediately took notice of Miranda as she crossed the floor, but she seemed unaware of the man's attention—of all men's attention. Miranda seemed to have no idea how lovely she was, how attractive she was . . . and how males responded to her.

It made Theo crazy. He didn't think he'd ever felt jealous over a woman in his life, but he felt it intensely whenever another man even glanced at Miranda.

She settled in and ordered a cosmopolitan, sipping it as she waited for Olivia to arrive. Olivia was keeping a secret from her best friend, Miranda. Olivia was a part-blood Tylwyth Teg with special abilities. And now that her mates had injected her with goblin blood, letting that blood transmute the fae blood she already possessed, she was immortal . . . or at least immortal by human standards. The fae did grow old and die eventually, but it took many, many centuries.

Theo knew how absolutely crazy all of that would seem to Miranda, yet she had a huge surprise coming. Not only was she the mate to two full-blooded Tylwyth Teg men . . . she was a part-blood Tylwyth Teg herself.

Theo ordered bourbon and sipped, keeping one eye on Miranda. Yes. This evening he would tell Marco. It was way past time.

Out of the corner of his eye, Theo noticed the black-haired man get up and approach Miranda. Every muscle in Theo's body went rigid. The man sidled up to the bar on her side and set his drink down. He said something and laughed, but Miranda just smiled politely and drew away from him a little. The man said something else and Miranda looked down at the bar and played with her glass, obviously trying not to encourage him. Her body language was clear, but the man seemed oblivious to it.

Theo couldn't take it any longer. He got up and crossed the floor toward them with his drink in hand. The black-haired man watched him approach with a belligerent look on his long face and a challenge in his eyes.

"Leave her alone," Theo growled as he walked toward them. "She doesn't want to talk to you."

"Theo!" Miranda cried, her beautiful eyes sparkling and her short blonde curls bouncing. "It's so good to see you." Theo could see she genuinely meant that. She turned to the man. "I'm sorry, could you please excuse us?"

The black-haired man looked chagrined and left them alone.

"Sit down," Miranda said, patting the seat the other man had vacated.

Theo slid in and set his glass on the bar.

"What are you doing here?" she asked.

Suddenly, he was at a loss, finding he couldn't lie to her. It wasn't like he visited the mall very often on his own. "I'm here to see you, of course," he answered with a grin.

She laughed. He loved the sound of it, so lilting and clear. There was something less happy in her eyes, however.

"Everything all right?" he asked.

She licked her lips. "You guys really weren't joking that day in the restaurant, were you? I've been . . . seeing things." She shook her head, letting her curls tumble around her face. "Strange things. I asked Olivia to come out with me today, so we could talk."

"You want to talk about this kind of stuff at the mall?"

"I wanted a little normality, I guess. I'm craving normality these days since I'm not sure exactly what normal is anymore." She fell silent and studied her glass with serious intent. "There are strange things in this world, aren't there? Things I never would've dreamed."

Theo could see it in her eyes and on her face; Miranda was struggling hard to understand the way reality had changed in the last couple of days and her place in this new world. He'd seen it before, people struggling with the concept that most of what they'd been told during their lives wasn't true.

"I understand," he replied in all truthfulness and took a drink of his bourbon. "Can I buy you another drink?" he asked, glancing at her empty cosmopolitan glass.

She looked regretful and shook her head no. "Sorry, I'm meeting Olivia soon. We've got an appointment for manicures." She smiled sadly and rolled her eyes. "All in the name of normality. She should be here any minute. After that we're going somewhere quiet to talk about . . . everything."

"I'm willing to discuss things with you too, Miranda." He leaned forward a little. "Would you like to have dinner with me sometime this week?" The question was out of his mouth before he realized he'd been asking it. Just then he saw Olivia enter the bar and spot them. "We could talk then," he finished.

Miranda smiled. "I'd love to," she answered in a warm voice. "I'm free tomorrow night if you'd like."

"How about I pick you up at eight?"

Miranda nodded. "I'll look forward to it."

Olivia reached them and kissed his cheek. "Theo! It's so good to see you."

"You too, Olivia." They'd just seen each other that morning actually. Theo was training Olivia in her Tylwyth Teg powers in order for her to take her place in the Gaelan triad along with Will and Mason. Miranda knew about none of that. Not yet.

"It's too bad we can't stay and talk more, but the manicurist awaits. Unless you want a manicure too, Theo?" she asked with a raised eyebrow and a twinkle in her eye.

He was almost tempted, if only to spend more time with Miranda, but he sensed Miranda needed Olivia's company more than his right now. Theo laughed. "Uh, no. Thanks."

"I didn't think so." Olivia looked at her best friend. "You ready, Miranda?"

Miranda slid off her stool and gathered her packages. "I'll see you tomorrow night, Theo."

"Tomorrow night?" Olivia questioned with a smile. "What's happening tomorrow night?" Theo heard her ask as they walked through the bar toward the door.

"He's taking me to dinner," Miranda answered with a smile.

As they left, Olivia shot a meaningful look over her shoulder at Theo and smiled.

Theo turned back to the bar and sipped his drink, deep in thought. Someone slid onto the stool next to him.

"Why didn't you tell me?" The voice was deep, ragged and tormented-sounding.

Marco.

Theo briefly closed his eyes before turning to look at him. Marco's blue eyes looked pensive. "I was going to tell you tonight. I'm sorry I kept it from you this long."

Without a word, Marco turned his gaze to the bartender and ordered a shot of tequila. He downed it quickly. "Damn" was all he said. He ordered another shot, drank that and stared at the empty glass. His dark hair fell into his eyes. "Damn," he repeated. "I can't fucking believe it."

"Why are you here, anyway?"

Marco's jaw locked for a moment before he spoke. "I knew it. Somehow I knew you'd found her. I followed you today to find out if I was right."

Theo sighed. "I'm sorry I kept her to myself for this time."

"I understand. I really do." He shrugged and grinned at him. "I would've done the same. Still, just being near her, seeing her . . . *damn*." He paused. "I have a powerful will to punch you out right now, friend."

"She has Tylwyth Teg blood. She just started seeing goblins, but it's all new to her and very confusing. That's why I didn't tell you. She needs time."

He let out a loud laugh. "Bullshit."

Theo played with his glass. "Yes, all right, perhaps there was an element of selfishness in there as well, but I'm serious. For all intents and purposes, she's human."

"So, basically, she knows nothing of our kind and she's mortal."

"Yes."

Marco gave a short, bitter laugh. "So, beyond the fact that there are two men bonded to her, there are some roadblocks."

"To say the least."

"I need to meet her, talk to her . . . touch her."

Jealousy flared in Theo. "I asked her to dinner tomorrow night. It wouldn't be good if you showed up. It might scare her off. She's in a delicate place right now."

"Theo." Marco was silent for several moments. "If you don't want to share her, expect competition." He got up and walked away.

# Two

NORMALITY.

That had become her internal refrain. Ever since she'd been a child that's what she'd wanted. She thought she'd finally had it, that she'd tamed the chaos that had been her life.

But it appeared that wasn't the case after all.

Normality. Stability. These things just weren't destined to be hers.

She would embrace the small bit of normal she did have, though, and get ready for her date, if it could be called that. Miranda guessed it was a date, at least. The attraction between them seemed to be mutual.

She'd had the hots for Theo from the first time she'd ever seen him. Tall, broad-shouldered and leanly muscled, the man was like a living, breathing god. It wasn't just his looks or his bone-meltingly sexy Welsh accent, it was his personality she found attractive. Theo was intelligent and witty. Someone you could have long conversations with . . . after he'd made you come hard enough to see stars.

Theo seemed, in a word, *perfect*.

Miranda stared into the mirror critically, and then applied a little more lipstick. She'd decided on a red skirt and top for the evening, along with her matching pair of heels that she'd bought at the mall the previous day. The outfit was sexy, yet not *too* sexy. She wanted to entice Theo, not make him think she'd do him on the first date.

Okay, so she actually might do him on the first date, but she didn't want *him* to know that.

This was all wonderfully normal. It had nothing to do with goblins, or the Tylwyth Teg. It was just her getting ready for a night out. Something she'd done many times before. She'd just disregard the fact that the date was with a five-hundred-year-old fae, according to Olivia.

She was so nervous her hands shook as she applied a little gloss over her lipstick. It had been a long time since she'd accepted a date with anyone she really liked, least of all with a man like Theo. Mostly, she just went out with men she knew she could never be serious with, just for fun. Commitments weren't her cup of tea. Never had been and probably never would be.

The fact that Theo wasn't human? She shook her head. She wouldn't think about that right now.

Theo was the kind of guy she could actually see having a relationship with, despite the weirdness she was trying not to think about. Although why she'd said yes to him, she wasn't sure. The man scared her and excited her at the same time. Yet, when he'd asked her out, she'd accepted so fast she'd barely known she'd done it.

The doorbell rang and Miranda practically jumped out of her skin. She primped one last time and went to answer it.

"Theo," she said smoothly, masking her nervousness. Wow, he looked good. He'd dressed in a well-tailored suit and wore a black dress coat. His long blond hair was tied at the nape of his neck, revealing the aristocratic bone structure of his face and his intense gray eyes. "You look incredible," she managed with a smile.

Olivia had told her that he and his partner, Marco, were the head honchos, the men in charge of the faction of Gaelans here in the city. Olivia hadn't met Marco, but Theo had the body and bearing to play such role. He was the epitome of grace and power and emanated control and self-possession. She could easily see how men would respect and obey him.

His gaze swept over her as she ushered him into her living room. God, he had a great ass. "As do you, Miranda. Though you always look beautiful."

She laughed. "You've only ever seen me a few times. You should see me when I wake up in the morning."

He held her gaze speculatively and smiled. She blushed crimson, realizing what he was probably thinking. Theo might like to see her when she'd just woken up . . . be there in the bed with her. Tingling excitement raced up her spine at the thought.

He leaned forward and inhaled near her throat. "You smell as good as you look too."

Had it suddenly grown hot in the room? "Thank you." She stared at him for a moment, and then went to the hall closet for her coat. "Well, I suppose we should get going."

He followed her and helped her on with her coat. His masculinity enveloped her and nearly took her breath away. His hands rested on her shoulder for a heartbeat before he moved away.

God, the man was a menace. The feel of his hands on her was enough to send her spiraling into every sexual fantasy she'd ever had about him. She'd had a bunch since she'd met him, when it was just her and her vibrator.

She turned and found him a breath's space away, looking at her with an intent expression. For a moment, she thought he would kiss her. Instead he went to the door and held it open for her.

Miranda felt a little disappointed that he hadn't kissed her, but she didn't let it show. She grabbed her purse from the nearby kitchen counter and walked out the door with Theo following.

They exited the building and got into Theo's silver BMW. On the way downtown they made nice chitchat—first date talk.

The restaurant he'd selected was very expensive, very high class. Miranda was glad she'd chosen the skirt, top and heels she wore. Just as they were opening the door another man approached them. He was tall, with dark hair and blue eyes. He wore a pair of black dress pants and a gray cashmere sweater under a long black duster.

The man was as drop-dead gorgeous as Theo. Miranda's mouth went dry, watching him approach. He walked with a sure, badass kind of swagger. Could this be Marco? It *felt* like Marco, but why she should think that escaped her.

"Theo!" the man said. "Hey, great to see you."

Theo pulled her against him a little and hesitated before answering. "Hey, Marco." He didn't sound incredibly enthusiastic. "Miranda, this is Marco Collins."

Marco stuck out his hand and Miranda took it. His touch sent shivers up her arm—honest-to-God vibrations skittering up her spine and through her body. "Nice to meet you, Miranda."

"Marco." She smiled. "I'm Miranda Davis." For some reason she felt compelled to make sure he knew her whole name. It was odd that she instantly liked this man. "I've heard a lot about you."

She had that same sense of *knowing* Marco, the way she'd had with Theo when she'd first met him. It was strange. Like she'd met him before and they'd been close, but she hadn't seen him in a really long time. She wanted to get to know him better, much more intimately, and not just on a physical level.

Miranda glanced at Theo, feeling the slightest bit guilty for being so attracted to his friend.

"Really?" He glanced at Theo. "I wonder what he's said." Miranda saw his eyes flash silvery and angry for a moment before returning to blue. "Are you two eating here?"

"Yes," answered Theo. He said no more.

Miranda frowned and shot him a look. How unfriendly he was being! "We have a reservation. I'm sure Theo wouldn't mind if we shared a table, would you, Theo?"

Theo glanced at her and hesitated, but recovered nicely. "No, of course not. You're welcome to share our table, Marco."

Marco shook his head. "No, I don't want to be a *third wheel*. You two are obviously on a date." He shot a hostile look at Theo, then took Miranda's hand and squeezed it gently. His touch sent shivers up her spine again. "I hope we meet again sometime soon."

"Uh, me too," Miranda managed to stutter out. She felt another twinge of guilt at being fascinated with the friend of the man she was currently on a date with, but she and Theo had no commitment. She liked Theo, but at this point, she had a right to feel attracted to anyone else she desired. Anyway, she didn't do commitments. She did affairs.

"Great, Marco. See you later then," said Theo as he guided her away with a possessive grip on her arm.

Miranda cast one more glance over her shoulder as Theo herded her through the doors of the restaurant. Marco stood on the sidewalk, watching her with a dark, intent gaze.

They were seated at a private table in the back that had been set with candles and flowers. A bottle of red wine already sat in a tall metal holder beside the table. It was beautiful and intimate. Obviously, Theo had requested this be done before they'd arrived. Miranda was quite flattered he'd gone to the trouble.

They settled in. The waiter poured the wine for them both, then left them to decide what they'd like to eat. Miranda decided on salmon in a rich cream sauce and some steamed vegetables. Theo ordered a steak.

"So," said Theo as they waited for their food to arrive, "how are you?"

Miranda knew he didn't mean just in general. She pursed her lips. "Aside from thinking I'm going nuts, I'm okay."

"Olivia thought she was nuts too."

Miranda nodded. "She told me about everything yesterday. How when she'd started coming into her abilities she'd withdrawn from everyone, thinking she was insane. She told me about Will and Mason and how they helped her to accept what was happening to her." She shrugged. "It's just all a little . . .

much. I've seen more, er, goblins since the night in the restaurant, but I guess I've been trying to ignore it all. It's so crazy and your mind can only take so much at one time."

"This world is filled with all kinds of things, Miranda, wild and unbelievable things. If you ignore your abilities and you ignore the truth, it will only make things harder for you in the long run. Do you understand?"

"Yes. I just wish for normality, I guess."

"Things will become normal again, but it will be a different kind of normal than you're used to."

Miranda laughed. "I guess."

"There are three kinds of goblins, did Olivia explain that to you?"

"A little."

"There are hobgoblins, who are always servants to the kingpin goblins. Those are the first two kinds. Last, there are the regular run-of-the-mill goblins. Sometimes they're servants to the kingpins and sometimes they just pass themselves off as humans, live under glamour their whole lives."

She frowned. "Why would they do that?"

"The goblins and the fae are vastly outnumbered by humans. It was not always so. Before, this world belonged to the Other-Kin. However, war and sickness almost killed us all off long ago. Now we live in the human world and most of us have learned to live by human rules."

"And some goblins and fae then interbreed with humans?"

Theo nodded. "Fertility is vastly diminished in a coupling like that, but it happens. You're an example. So is Olivia."

"But you're a full-blood. So, tell me about yourself."

He leaned forward, his gray eyes sparkling. "I'd much rather hear about you, love."

Miranda shrugged. "I'm kind of boring."

Theo smiled. "Now, I know that isn't true. Are you from the city?"

She shook her head. "I moved here with my mom from California when I was a teenager. She was escaping my father, who was abusive." She put a hand to her mouth. "I'm sorry, I wasn't going to tell you that. It just slipped out."

"Why wouldn't you tell me that?"

"It's a little heavy for a first date, that's all."

Theo leaned forward and took her hand. She had the same kind of reaction to Theo that she'd had with Marco. Little shivers of pleasure shook through her body at his touch. "I know we only just met, but I think we can skip the small talk and just be honest with each other. Let's both face the truth together."

A flicker of fear ran through Miranda. Wow. Theo was looking for something serious, wasn't he? She licked her lips and glanced away. "Okay."

It was true she did feel really comfortable with Theo. So comfortable, she'd let something slip that caused her a lot of pain, something she normally didn't tell anyone. That was odd.

"My mother had to run from my father," she continued, not even knowing why she did so. "We had to hide from him. He was very . . . violent."

"Were you successful? Did he ever find you?"

Miranda bit her lip and looked away, feeling her eyes fill up with tears. "Yes, he found us. That was how my mother died. I was eighteen and had pushed my mom to leave my dad. I convinced her to move all the way across the country, but he still found us." She dropped her gaze and studied the white table-cloth. "He, uh, killed himself afterward. I was there when it all happened."

Theo rubbed his thumb over the back of her hand to give her comfort. "I'm sorry, I can tell this gives you a lot of pain to discuss. We can change the subject, if you'd like."

Miranda shook her head and plunged ahead. "I was there when it happened," she repeated. She paused. "He kept saying he loved her." Her voice broke on the words as she remembered that day. "He told her he loved her while he . . ."

"I'm sorry."

"You never would've guessed it, looking at us as a family. Both my parents were professionals—my mother was a CPA, my father was an architect. People have a tendency to stereotype wife beaters, but my father broke all of the stereotypes." She shook her head. "You never would've guessed."

"Did he ever beat *you*, Miranda?" Theo asked gently.

She shook her head. "No. My mother was always the focus of his anger, not me."

"You were eighteen when this happened. What did you do after that?"

"I was already accepted to Newville State. In the fall, I went to college. I ended up getting a master's degree in psychology. Now I counsel women down at the local shelter." She shrugged. "There's not much money in it, but it's what I want to do. What do you do? I mean, I know you work with Will and Mason, but I don't know exactly what your job is."

"Marco and I head up things in this area."

"Big boss, huh?"

He smiled. "We're more like middle management in the whole scheme of things. We're both on a little"— he paused— "vacation from our duties right now. We have some personal issues to resolve."

"And Marco is your partner?"

Theo's face tightened a little. "Yes."

"Interesting! Yet, you don't seem to like him very much."

Their food arrived. Once they'd settled into eating their delicious meals—Miranda thought she'd have an orgasm right at the table, her salmon was so good—Theo shook his head. "It's not that I don't like him. I do like Marco very much. In fact, he's my best friend. It's just that we're currently having a small disagreement."

"Really? Over what? That is, if you don't mind me asking."

"No, I don't mind. We're having trouble agreeing on how to handle something very, very important to the both of us. Something very personal." He shrugged. "And I guess we're both feeling a little territorial."

Miranda took a sip of her wine. She could feel herself going into counselor mode. "Well, if you're best friends, and this thing means so much to the both of you, you have to find a way to compromise. To share. You have to find some common ground and learn to respect each other's claim."

Theo lifted a brow. "Did you learn that in kindergarten?"

Miranda laughed. "It is kind of elementary."

Theo nodded. "And yet you're right. You're totally right." He reached across the table and took her hand again. His gaze turned serious and intense. "I like you very much, Miranda."

She squeezed his hand. "I like you too."

"What do you want out of life?"

She smiled. "There's a complicated question."

"If money were no object, what would your life look like?" He released her hand and began eating again.

She paused. "If all my dreams came true? I'd have stability, normality. I'd live in the country, in a big log cabin surrounded by trees and greenery. I'd be able to start my own women's shelter and man it with skilled, caring people." She shrugged and smiled. "I'd have a husky. I love huskies. Maybe some horses."

"Sounds nice."

"I think so. So, tell me a little about yourself. Where are you from?"

"Wales, originally. From a very small village."

"Really. Do you speak Welsh?"

He nodded. "I do. It's the language of my ancestors. It's important for me to be fluent in it, in all the languages of my ancestors. I'm fluent in the old language of the Tylwyth Teg as well."

Miranda suddenly became very interested in her wineglass. "It was a very long time ago that you left Wales, wasn't it?"

"Yes," he replied carefully. "Are you becoming frightened again, love?"

She glanced up at him. "No, of course not."

"Please don't lie to me."

She licked her lips. "Well, can you blame me?"

Theo set down his fork and leaned forward. She felt his warm hand cover hers and she shuddered with pleasure. "Trust me when I say I'm young for my kind, Miranda. I don't have gray hair and the last time I checked, I didn't need Viagra."

Miranda laughed in surprise, looked up and got lost in his warm gaze. God, she really felt the need to test out that statement. Her mirth died in the face of the smoldering look in his eyes.

She cleared her throat and glanced away. "So, you're a five-hundred-year-old fae who has dedicated his life to fighting goblins," she said lightly with a raised eyebrow. "Got any hobbies?"

Theo laughed and leaned back in his chair. "Actually, I do. I'm a hobbyist photographer."

"Really?"

"I started right when the technology was first developing. I was entranced by it. I still am."

She took a sip of her wine. "Why?"

Theo considered her for a moment, deep in thought. The way he looked at her made her stomach do curious flip-flops and warmed her blood. There was emotion in his gaze when he looked at her, deep emotion. She'd always noticed it because it had always been there, ever since the first time she'd met him. It was there every time he looked at her.

"When you live so long and have watched so many lives pass away before you, when you watch history change, governments reach their summits and then fall, you start to see the impermanence of things. You learn to live in the moment, to appreciate beauty, no matter how ordinary it is. Photographs let you capture that and hang on to it for a time. It's comforting."

She was lost in his gaze, totally enraptured. "I see," she replied softly.

"Take that couple to our right, for example," he said.

Miranda looked over to see an older silver-haired gentleman

and an older woman. Rings glittered on their hands and she assumed they were married.

"Look at their body posture. Both of them are leaning toward each other, immersed in the other's smile, words and eyes. How long have they been married, a day? Forty years? We don't know any of that. All we know is that they're in love. This restaurant barely even seems to exist for them. All that exists is each other."

Suddenly the scene, which had seemed unremarkable before, seemed incredibly intimate—like she'd just caught the couple with their clothes off. Miranda looked away, back at Theo. He had seen splendor and truth in the most ordinary of things and he'd made her see it too. How remarkable.

Theo held her gaze for several heartbeats before speaking. "You see? *Beautiful.*"

Miranda understood he wasn't talking about just the scene he'd shown her.

"Want to get out of here?" he asked in a low voice that sounded like liquid velvet pouring over her skin.

Miranda barely found herself able to nod.


AS IF IN SOME MOVIE, they fell through his front door kissing. She couldn't get enough of the taste of him, the feel of his hands on her. Fumbling, laughing, they undressed each other. No way were they going to make it to an actual bed.

Miranda caught only glimpses of Theo's living room as they made their way toward the couch. Noting the décor in the half-light wasn't her priority at the moment, but it was tasteful and rich-looking. She noticed that much.

She finally got the last of Theo's shirt buttons undone and she almost purred as she ran her hands over the hard, warm and leanly muscled expanse of his chest. His fingers fumbled for her bra hook in the front.

"We really shouldn't be doing this," Theo whispered.

"I know," she answered breathlessly as he eased her down onto the couch. "This is crazy. I barely know you."

"There are so many things to consider," said Theo in between kisses. "There are . . . other people to think about. I'm doing this wrong, but, God, I can't stop myself." He finally got the front clasp of her bra undone and covered her nipple with his mouth.

Miranda arched with pleasure at the sensation of his lips around that so sensitive part of her body. He laved over it as he worked her red skirt down over her hips, then shifted and gave the other nipple the same treatment. Suddenly she lost the ability to form coherent thoughts.

They stopped talking.

Somehow they both managed to get most of their clothes off—the important articles, anyway. Miranda's fancy red top was unbuttoned and open, but not off. She was still wearing her heels. Theo's shirt was also unbuttoned and open, but not off.

None of that mattered now. Miranda's whole reality narrowed to the feel of his warm, hard-yet-soft body rubbing against her skin. She ran her hands over him, exploring the way the muscles of his back bunched as he moved, his lean hips and strong thighs.

God, she wanted to lick every inch of him, worship him.

Theo kissed his way down her stomach and eased her thighs

apart. She sank her fingers into his long hair, pulling it from the tie at the nape of his neck. Slowly, softly, he ran the tip of his tongue over her inner thigh—right at the tender place where it met her sex. Miranda was already excited, and this just poured fuel on the fire. He tormented her a moment longer, then slid his tongue in to lick her clit. It was swollen and sensitive.

Miranda moaned long and low as Theo teased it with his tongue.

"Miranda, you taste every bit like I thought you would." Theo groaned deep in his throat. He braced her legs open with strong hands and fastened his mouth over her for a longer taste.

Miranda arched her back and hung on for dear life as Theo licked her from perineum to clit with long strokes of his tongue. Dear God, he'd had a long time to learn the right way to go down on a woman, and he'd learned well. He spread her labia with his thumbs and laved the very heart of her, easing his tongue into her tight, aroused entrance.

"Theo," Miranda called in a breathless voice as he gently fucked her there, easing in and out of her the way she imagined his cock would. He moved up and pulled her swollen clit between his lips to massage it. His fingers replaced his tongue deep inside her, pushing her and pulling her straight toward a mind-blowing climax. She could feel herself wet between her thighs, drenching his pistoning fingers.

"Ride my fingers, love," came his deep voice from the darkness. He sounded incredibly aroused, his voice deep and thick. "I want to watch you."

She moved her hips, doing as he asked, sliding herself up and down on his fingers as he watched. Their breathing was the only sound in the room, along with the soft sound of her cunt not wanting to give up the penetration on every outward movement.

She'd never been so desperate for a man in her life. Never had she felt this aroused. She'd do anything to have him inside her. Common sense flickered, but was quickly squelched. It flickered again and she grabbed on to it with both hands. And, God, she wanted him *now*.

"Theo . . . condom," she managed to gasp. "Please."

He stopped and looked up at her. Shadows of the room played over his handsome face. "No need, love. Not with my kind."

She licked her lips and nodded. He crawled up her body, threaded his fingers through the hair at the nape of her neck and brought her mouth an inch from his. "I want you," he growled. "More than anything. Nothing can stop this now."

She couldn't even muster the words to agree with him.

He eased his lips over hers softly, teasing. Then he cupped her cheek and took her mouth, parting her lips and easing his tongue inside to glide and rub sensually against hers. She could taste the very faint flavor of herself on his tongue.

He eased his hands down to her hips and pulled her toward him, moving her so her ass was just on the very edge of the couch. It was the perfect height for him, where he knelt on the carpet in front of her.

The smooth head of his cock nudged the opening of her cunt. Miranda rolled her hips forward, wanting him inside her, wanting to be impaled. He entered her in a slow thrust, pushing the head just past her entrance.

She gasped as the width of him stretched her muscles.

"God, you're tight, love," Theo murmured against her lips. "How long has it been?"

His voice felt like silk on her skin, making her shiver. "A-a while. Why . . . is it bad?"

"Oh, no. It's not bad. You're sweet, hot and sweet." He groaned. "You're perfect, tight and excited. Fucking perfect."

Theo pushed in little by little, slowly letting her have an inch of him at a time. Miranda wanted to scream. He filled her so well, stretching her muscles and possessing her utterly. She rolled her hips, wanting all of him in her now, faster and harder, but Theo held on to her. He rocked back out, making sure she was lubricated enough—she was—and then slid in again. Finally he was seated within her to the base of his cock.

Theo stayed that way, completely sunk within her body and staring down at her in the half-light. Miranda thought she'd get lost in his eyes. He reached up and moved a tendril of hair away from her face in such a gesture of love and caring that it made tears prick her eyes. Theo kissed her forehead, then dropped down and kissed her possessively on the lips, taking her mouth with an aggressiveness that made Miranda cream anew, made her whimper in her throat.

Then he cupped her ass and started to move.

Miranda gasped and hit his shoulder with her fist. "Yes," she hissed. "God, that's what I wanted."

Theo groaned and started to thrust harder and faster. Miranda couldn't think, couldn't speak. The feel of his length and width inside her was almost beyond what she could handle.

"I'm coming," she whispered. Her climax skittered through

her body, built and threatened to explode. She tipped her head back and moaned. "Oh, don't stop. Don't stop!"

"No way," Theo gritted out.

The climax came up from the very depths of her. It overwhelmed everything. She could feel the muscles of her cunt convulsing around Theo's pistoning length, milking him. The pleasurable waves filled her, took the very breath from her. She couldn't scream, couldn't moan, couldn't do anything but lose herself to it. Miranda had never had a more intense sexual experience in her life.

Theo groaned and threw his head back. She could feel his cock jerk a little inside her as he came. It was erotic, so incredibly erotic watching this man come inside her. She loved knowing she'd given him as much pleasure as he'd given her.

They stayed wrapped around each other, breathing heavily. Miranda could feel herself trembling, not just from the physical exertion but from the pleasure she'd experienced. Her body still hummed and pulsed from it.

Theo found her mouth and kissed her deeply as he stroked her body with his broad skillful hands, making her sigh and shiver. They wallowed in the aftermath of their shared climax, joined at mouth and sex. He still hadn't gone soft inside her and she could feel her muscles rippling around his length.

Without a word, he wrapped her in his arms and pulled her off the couch onto the very soft, plush living room rug. They lay, still half dressed and panting, in the afterglow.

Miranda couldn't remember the last time sex had been this good.

Theo turned over and pulled her against him, scattered kisses over her cheeks and throat. Sated and deeply content, she wrapped her arms around him, seeking his warmth. With care, he removed the rest of her clothing—her shirt, bra and her heels.

She sat up and pushed his shirt over his shoulders, then let her fingers trail down over his very, very lovely chest and washboard abs. She'd always been a sucker for an accent and a nice chest. Theo had both.

"That was incredible," Theo murmured.

"It was."

He kissed her lingeringly and guided her hand to his cock. It was already getting hard again. "I want you again, love. Stay the night?"

She bit her lip. "Uh, well, I won't leave now, if that's what you're worried about." Staying the night . . . she wasn't sure she could do that. Miranda shivered a little, feeling the cool air touch her bare skin.

Theo took her hand from his chest, kissed her fingers and got to his feet. He pulled a blanket from the back of the couch and laid it over her. It was soft and Theo's scent clung to the material. Sighing, Miranda tucked herself up against the couch.

"Wait here a minute," he said.

Oh, she had a nice view as he walked away. She tipped her head to the side and admired.

He came back with two glasses of champagne and a large pillow. He slipped the pillow behind her back and he settled in beside her under the blanket. There were logs already in the wood-burning fireplace. He looked at them and they ignited.

"Uh, wow," Miranda said. In the face of that, intelligent conversation failed her.

"One of the nice things about being with you is that I can be myself."

"So, you have . . . magick?"

"I'm a full-blood Tylwyth Teg, Miranda. We have magick, though different fae have different skills. A lot of it has to do with genetics. Some skills can be learned as well."

"Olivia said that Will is a part-blood and doesn't have magick. She says Mason isn't Tylwyth Teg at all. He's part shape shifter . . . dragon breed. It all seems so unreal, and I can almost dismiss it as craziness, then I see one of those things, or you start a fire without even touching it." She paused and smiled a little. "Although I guess you started a fire in me long before you ever touched me."

"I did?"

"It was the way you looked at me." She shivered. "From day one you looked at me like you wanted me." She shook her head. "No, not even that. You looked at me like I was already yours."

Theo remained quiet for a long moment.

"Why do you think that might be?" she pressed.

Theo picked up his glass and took a long sip of champagne. He set down the glass and looked at her. "Because you *are* mine, Miranda. Mine in a very fundamental way. I think maybe I knew that on some level from the moment I first saw you."

Miranda swallowed hard and glanced away. Sometimes commitment felt like a noose tightening around her throat. Even though she knew that her mother's life was not her own, images from her past crowded her mind. Though she'd dealt with what had happened, ghosts still haunted her.

She gave a light laugh that came out sounding forced. "You

seem pretty sure of yourself, there, buddy. I mean, the sex was pretty amazing, but—"

"There are things you don't know yet, Miranda."

"More things?" Miranda took a long drink of her champagne. She needed it. It was cold, sweet and a little tart.

"How much did Olivia tell you about her relationship with Will and Mason?"

Miranda took a moment to reflect. "She said they had a lot in common. She said that they shared a lot, the three of them, related to their abilities."

"That's it?"

"Yes. She's not the type to kiss and tell. She doesn't tell me the intimate stuff. That's private."

Theo laughed, and then swore softly under his breath in a language she didn't understand. "Obviously, she intended for me to do that part," he muttered.

"What? What part?"

He turned and took the glass from her hand and set it on the floor. Miranda looked up at him in confusion. He stared into her eyes with that unsettling yet lovely way of his. "Miranda, this is all going much faster than I ever intended. There are things I have to tell you and it's better I don't put them off."

"Uh, okay."

"When you first met me, what did you think?"

She smiled and glanced away. *Hot guy, two o'clock,* that's what she'd thought. Yet, there was more than just that superficial attraction. There always had been. "Well, beyond that I was attracted to you physically, I felt in some way that I'd met you before, or that we'd known each other for a very long time. I wanted to be with you, get to know you. But I don't mean just on some shallow level, I mean really grow close to you. I wanted to share things about myself with you that I normally never reveal." She shrugged. "My reaction was strange, but you asked for honesty back in the restaurant. I'm giving it."

"There's a reason you felt that way about me, Miranda. Now I'm asking for complete honesty again. How did you feel when you met Marco earlier this evening?"

Her brow furrowed. She couldn't figure out where all this was going. "Uh, truthfully?"

Theo nodded. "You can say anything. It won't hurt my feelings."

"Okay. At first glance, I thought he was one of the hottest men I'd ever seen, with maybe the exception of you. After that, I felt the same way about him as I felt about you the first time we met. I felt a yearning to know him better, a deep need. When he left us, I was . . . disappointed."

She bit her lip. Had she really said any of that out loud? Miranda watched Theo's face carefully for signs of anger.

Theo only smiled a little and nodded. "Yes. I'm not surprised you felt that way. Thank you for being honest."

"What do you mean?" she asked, irritated. He was hiding something. "Just be straight with me instead of dancing around whatever it is you have to say!"

"Okay." He drew a breath. "You deserve honesty. You're my mate. Not only are you my mate, you're Marco's mate as well."

Miranda fell silent, processing what he'd just said. Then she laughed. "You're joking. Mates? What are we . . . friends somewhere in Australia . . . or animals?"

"Not animals, we're Tylwyth Teg. Can I explain?"

Miranda was busy sucking down the rest of her champagne in big gulps. She waved her hands at him to continue, not really sure how many more revelations she could take. Her reality had already changed so much.

"The Tylwyth Teg and OtherKin who bind themselves to our cause work in groups of three. Initially, the Tylwyth Teg psychics find two individuals who are mystically bonded, for example, Will and Mason, or me and Marco. The bonding goes past simple compatibility. It goes much deeper than that. It's an actual compatibility of the patterns of our spirits."

"So you're like . . . lovers?"

Theo shook his head. "No, not myself and Marco or Will and Mason. Although it has been known to happen with same-sex pairs. Anyway, there is a third. Sometimes the third is found right away and sometimes it takes centuries. The psychics found Olivia for Will and Mason." He paused. "But I found you."

"So it's some kind of mystical dating service?"

Theo laughed. "No, not really."

"So let me get this straight: you found me for you and . . . for Marco?" She said uncertainly, fear tingeing her words.

"United as a triad, we will be stronger and more powerful. This is the way of our kind. Do you know all the meanings of the word *triad*? It means three people or things that are connected, but it also means three musical notes." He paused. "The three of us together would be harmony."

Miranda realized she was gripping the stem of her champagne glass so hard she might break it. She set it on the carpet beside her. "So what would Marco think of what just happened between us?"

Theo's mouth tightened as he looked away. "He's going to be angry with me, and he's going to be jealous."

Miranda sat for a moment, trying to get a handle on things. With everything that had happened to her in the last couple days, this was the icing on top of the cake of her suddenly changed world.

"So," she began, "this is what Olivia, Will and Mason have?"

"Yes."

"So, I'm meant to be with both you and Marco . . . both of you. Maybe even together? At the same time?"

"That depends on you."

"Will there be . . . love?"

"Usually," he said carefully, "in a pairing or threesome where there's sexual attraction, there is deep, deep love and incredible commitment."

It was too much, way too much for her to handle at that moment.

Not only was the world nothing like she'd grown up believing, she didn't know her place in it. That normality and stability she'd been trying so hard to achieve all her life was slipping through her fingers so fast she couldn't even grab the tail of it.

On top of all that—if that wasn't enough—not only had one man laid claim to her, but *two*. Miranda shuddered. She wasn't ready to commit to one man, let alone . . .

Miranda pushed the blanket aside, rose and sought her clothes. "I've got to go."

Theo stood. Miranda tried not to look at him in all his naked grace. Even flaccid his cock was beautiful, and the lines of his body beckoned to be explored.

Such a pity he was pushing her too hard.

Confusion and pain were clear in his eyes; she tried not to look at them while she dressed. "Don't go, Miranda," he said.

"Have to."

"You don't have your car. Let me take you home."

"No!" She turned to him. "No. I'll get the doorman downstairs to call me a cab." Miranda grabbed her purse and, while still buttoning her shirt, walked toward the door.

"Miranda, please wait."

She shook her head. Miranda reached the door and turned to him before she opened it. "You're a great guy, Theo. I like you a lot." Her voice broke. "This is just too much for me right now. Give me some time?"

Theo stood staring at her. He didn't say a word.

She left him like that.

# THREE

THEO WALKED INTO HIS DARK APARTMENT and set his keys down in the multicolored ceramic bowl near his answering machine. He had no messages. It had been three days and he'd heard nothing from Miranda.

Damn.

The hair prickled along his arms and at the back of his neck, letting him know he wasn't alone. His head jerked up and his gaze centered on the dark form sitting in a chair in the living room.

"You fucking slept with her," came Marco's low, angry voice.

"Marco—"

Marco was out of the chair and on him before he could utter his next word. Theo slammed back against the phone table under Marco's weight.

Marco grabbed Theo's shirt and dragged him up against his chest. "You fucking slept with her, you bastard," Marco growled and slammed his fist into Theo's face. Blinding white-hot pain blossomed across his cheekbone and over his temple. He tasted coppery blood on his tongue.

Rage erupted in Theo. In a burst of strength, he pushed Marco back and snarled, *"Hie beaucahm!"* Stop now! There was no sense in fighting. They were evenly matched in most every way, magickally and physically. It would be a draw. There was no point. Anyway, he didn't want to fight his best friend.

Marco stilled at the use of the old language. He backed away warily, a violent expression on his face. "I can feel the residual emotion in here. I know you did."

Theo put a hand to his aching face. "Yes," he said calmly. "I slept with her. I'm sorry, but I don't regret it."

He watched Marco uneasily. He'd never seen his partner this way. Marco seemed to seethe with rage and frustration. "You need to back the fuck off for a while, my friend," he growled. "You are getting entirely too possessive."

Theo shook his head, gingerly touching his cheek where he was sure a bruise was already showing itself. "She's not ready for us, Marco. Not for either of us, certainly not both of us to-gether."

"Fuck you!"

Theo looked up, half amused, half pissed off. "Excuse me?"

"You're just saying that so I'll ease off you and give you more time alone with her."

Theo sighed. "Look, Marco. I told her about the bonding and she fled my apartment like I'd just told her she was going to die of cancer or something."

"You told her *after* you slept with her."

"Focus, Marco! You're missing the point. Yes, I told her after I slept with her. My tale of OtherKin bonding scared her. The whole of it frightened her to bits, especially the part where I said she was bonded to both of us and likely love and commitment would follow."

"Fuck."

"Yeah." He sighed. "Fuck. She hasn't called me in three days."

Marco walked over and slumped down onto the couch. "So now what?"

Theo flicked the lights on with his mind, bathing his cream and blue living room in a soft glow. "Now you go to see her. Maybe your charms will be more persuasive than mine were."

Marco shot him a dirty look.

"I'm serious, Marco. I'm backing off, giving you room to woo." He waved his hand. "So, go . . . woo." The thought of Marco with Miranda set his teeth on edge, made jealousy rise, but he needed to tamp it down. They couldn't do this. He sighed and touched his face. "That's what you want, right?"

"Yeah."

"Go see her tomorrow at work. She's got to be feeling the bond a little. I know she's attracted to both of us. I don't think she'll reject you."

Marco grinned arrogantly. "She won't reject me."

Theo smiled in spite of himself. "Well, if you're so sure, go find out. Just don't push too hard, all right?"

Marco got up and started walking toward the door. He turned before he left. "Sorry about punching you."

"Hey, believe me, sleeping with Miranda was worth it."

Rage briefly passed over Marco's face, then he turned and left. Theo sat for a while in his living room nursing his swelling face and trying not to think about Marco's hands on Miranda, her sighs, her moans all for him . . . and failing.

MIRANDA TOOK HER BAG FROM THE YOUNG KID at the end of the checkout, mumbled thanks and walked toward the exit. She walked with her head down, deep in thought. She was on her break and had several more counseling appointments that afternoon. She didn't feel at her best, however, and was considering taking the rest of the day off. Her clients deserved more from her than she felt able to give today, but they had no one but her. Really, she ought to try and stick it out.

A man stepped in front of her and she raised her head to go around him. Her eyes widened and she dropped her bag. Cans of soup and the sundries she'd purchased rolled out onto the floor.

Goblin.

The goblin stared at her in confusion for a moment before realization dawned. He smiled, revealing blackened teeth. "You can see me," he murmured. "The real me."

A clerk hurried over to help her gather her things. "I don't know what you're talking about. You just startled me. I'm sorry," she mumbled at the goblin as she knelt to aid the clerk. She really needed to learn how to quit dropping things whenever she saw a goblin. It was becoming a frequent occurrence these days.

"Riiiight," drawled the goblin.

Miranda paused in the process of gathering cans and stared at the floor as the goblin walked away, laughing softly under his breath.

"What a jerk," the clerk said as he handed her the refilled bag. "He made you drop your bag and then he laughed about it."

She gave the clerk a forced smile. "Yeah, what a jerk," she agreed in a shaky-sounding voice. She took the bag and made a hasty retreat back across the street to the center.

Valerie, the volunteer manning the front counter, buzzed her through the security door. It opened into a large common room with sofas and a television set. In the back of the building there were rooms where the women and their children stayed, a playroom and a cafeteria. Miranda walked toward the offices off the common room. She had time for a quick bite before her next appointment.

She'd just finished washing down her last bit of sandwich with some spring water when she heard a timid knock on her door. Miranda glanced at her watch and frowned. It wasn't time for her next appointment yet. "Come in," she called.

Sarah, one of the women taking refuge at the center, stepped inside. "Hi, Miss Davis."

"Hi, Sarah. What's up?"

Sarah twisted her hands in front of her. "Do you have a minute to talk?"

"Sure. Sit down."

Sarah sat down on the edge of the worn green sofa opposite Miranda's desk. The woman always looked uneasy, like a wild animal about to bolt. "He's been hanging around, Miss Davis," she said in a quavering voice. Her brown eyes were wide and her hands were white and shaking in her lap. "Hanging around the center, on the street."

Miranda didn't have to ask whom she spoke of. "Okay. How

many times have you seen him?" Restraining orders frequently meant little to abusive husbands.

"Yesterday morning. I didn't go to work because I was afraid he was out there . . . watching for me. Then I saw him again today." She inhaled noisily. "He's out there now," she finished with a rush of exhaled air.

"It's okay, Sarah. You're safe here." She reached for the phone. "I'll call Craig. He'll come down and take care of it." Craig was one of the police officers who regularly kept an eye on the center. The police couldn't be here twenty-four-seven, but the station was just down the street. They'd have a cop here in no time.

She'd no sooner dialed the number when she heard a crash come from the receiving area.

"*Sarah!*" a man yelled.

Sarah stiffened. "Oh, God. It's Brian."

The intercom on her desk came on. "Miranda," came Valerie's voice. "We've got a problem."

"I'm calling the police now," she answered.

Quickly, Miranda told the police they needed someone *right now* and hung up the phone. She turned to Sarah. "You stay here, all right?"

Sarah nodded.

Miranda turned and went quickly for the receiving area. Her pulse raced furiously. This didn't happen often, but when it did . . .

She opened the security door to find Valerie standing at the counter looking supremely pissed off. Miranda sucked in a breath when she caught sight of the man.

Brian was the goblin from the grocery store.

She mastered her reaction as best she could at that terrible surprise. In his fist, Brian held some flowers. He'd probably been at the grocery store to buy them. Behind him Miranda could see he'd tipped over a stand of brochures and educational leaflets. That had been the crash she'd heard.

"You?" the goblin said. "You're the damn counselor who's been telling my Sarah not to come home to me?" He took a menacing step toward her.

Crap. All she had to do was hang on until the police got here. It wouldn't be long.

"Sarah is making her own choices now," Miranda replied steadily, feeling a rush of anger and fear surge through her body. "You need to leave. *Now.*" The trick was not to engage him in conversation, just persuade him to leave. Firmly.

"No, I'm not leaving until I see Sarah. She needs me. *I love her.*"

Miranda remembered how Sarah had come to them, bruised, with hospital dressings. She'd had quite a history at the local emergency room—lots of accidental falls and mysterious injurious mishaps. Sarah had been afraid Brian would eventually kill her, so she'd come to the center. She expressed fear of Brian, and absolutely no inclination of returning to him. Brian had beaten all the love out of that relationship.

Sarah wanted a new life, a new fear-free life, just like Miranda's mother had wanted but had never achieved. Miranda would do all she could to ensure that Sarah got that.

Brian took another step toward her and Miranda said a little prayer that the cops would show soon. She'd taken self-defense classes, but she didn't want to have to use what she'd learned . . .

especially not on a goblin. How strong were they anyway? She had a feeling much stronger than a human.

"Bitch, stop looking at the door and start looking at me!" he growled.

Brian bum-rushed her and Miranda dodged to the side, avoiding him. He came at her again, grabbing her around her middle and pressing her up against his chest.

Everything Miranda had learned came rushing to the fore. She brought her elbow back sharp and hard into his ribs. Brian grunted and released her. She turned and punched him in the Adam's apple before he could react. He gagged and backed away, hand to his throat.

She stood back, breathing hard and shaking. Nice to see the techniques worked on goblins. Her hand hurt like hell, though.

Movement flickered in the corner of her eye and she saw a man dressed in a long black coat rush into the room. At first she thought it was a cop—but cops didn't dress in long black coats and leather boots. Then she recognized Marco.

Marco grabbed Brian faster than she could blink and strong-armed the goblin out the door. She heard a couple of grunts that were quickly drowned out by wailing sirens. Miranda glanced at Valerie, who was white and shaking, and then went for the door. By the time Miranda got outside, the police were there, breaking up the fight.

The cops had both men in custody. Brian was fighting two police officers, but Marco wasn't resisting Craig, who held him by the upper arm.

"Wait," Miranda called to Craig as she ran to them. "Let him go. He was just helping me out."

Craig released Marco. "What happened, Miranda?"

"That man, his name is Brian Simpson. He was attempting to contact his wife, who is staying with us. He was abusive and belligerent and grabbed me with an intent to harm."

"You want to press charges?"

She glanced at Brian, who was giving her one hell of an evil eye. "Oh, yeah," she answered him. "I do." There was no doubt about that.

Craig rocked back on his heels. "All right. We'll arrest scumbag over there. Come on down to the station as soon as you can."

Miranda nodded shakily and watched Craig walk over to cuff Brian and read him his rights. Brian kept his threatening stare centered on her the whole time.

She felt Marco's warm hand close over her arm. "Come on. I don't like the way he's looking at you." His touch sent shivers through her body and broke the stunned trance she'd slipped into.

Miranda looked up at him. "Thank you." She sucked in a breath as she saw the bleeding cut above his eye.

"You don't need to thank me. I'm just glad the police got there when they did. I had a powerful need to kill that goblin for laying his hands on you."

He led her toward the entrance of the center. Brian started yelling obscenities at them. "You don't even know what you are, bitch!" He yelled.

Miranda shivered and Marco quickly ushered her through the door.

"You saw what he was?" she asked as they entered the center. Valerie was busy picking up all the scattered brochures. Miranda shut up so they wouldn't say anything to freak Valerie out.

"Yeah," he said, glancing at Valerie and cutting off the rest of his sentence. "Bastard."

Miranda's jaw locked when she glimpsed the crushed bouquet of flowers on the floor. She picked it up and tossed it in the trash can near the counter.

Miranda turned. "Valerie, this is a friend of mine, Marco Collins."

Valerie gave him a once over and raised a brow. "Nice to meet you, Marco, and, hey, thanks for your help."

"Not a problem," he responded. He smiled and it sent butterflies through Miranda's stomach. His smile revealed straight white teeth and made his eyes sparkle. "I have to say it was a pleasure, really."

"I need to go down and press charges against him at the station," Miranda said to Valerie.

"I'll come with you," answered Marco.

She turned to him and looked at his forehead. "You need to have that looked at. It looks like it needs stitches."

"I'm coming with you."

"You need to go the emergency room. That needs—"

"Miranda. I'm coming with you to the police station." His tone of voice persuaded her not to argue.

Miranda snapped her mouth closed.

Valerie nudged her. "Let the pretty man go with you," she muttered. "What's wrong with you?"

Miranda pressed her lips into a thin line. "Give me a few minutes to go talk with Sarah and cancel my afternoon appointments. Wait here?" she asked Marco.

"Of course."

Miranda was sure Valerie would be eating out of Marco's hand by the time she returned.

AFTER THEY'D FINISHED AT THE POLICE STATION, Miranda hustled Marco off to the emergency room. He sat on a silver table while a doctor stitched up the deep split above his eye. Miranda stood near him.

"I wish we could have met for the second time under different circumstances," said Marco, while the doctor finished up.

"I don't know. I'm pretty glad you showed up when you did."

"You looked like you could handle yourself."

She smiled. "I've never actually had to defend myself before. I hope it's not the start of a trend."

"Me too," he answered. He hesitated, and then added, "Keep me and Theo around and we'll make sure it won't be."

The doctor finished and gave Marco some parting instructions. As she did so, Miranda considered him. Physically, he was a little shorter than Theo and a bit more on the muscular side. Theo was leanly muscular, whereas Marco was broader of shoulder and a bit more ripped. Marco's hair was  dark, about collar-length. His eyes were almond shaped and a lovely, clear blue. Marco's deep, sexy-rough voice was accent-free. He sounded one-hundred-percent American.

He was different from Theo in more than just physical ways. She didn't know either of them well, but she had enough information so far to make that determination. Theo was all cool, controlled power, where Marco seemed to run hotter and faster. Marco reminded her more of a badass James Dean type. Perhaps Marco was a bit more reckless, though it had been Theo, apparently, who'd preempted Marco where she was concerned.

The doctor gathered her things, and Marco slid off the counter and came to stand in front of Miranda. "I'd like to talk," he said.

She didn't answer. She just reached up and drew her finger over the thin white scar that marked the skin under his left eye. He closed his eyes at her touch and that now-familiar tingle ran up her arm. "You'll have another scar from today to match this one."

"It will be worth it."

"Worth it? Why?" she asked.

"Since I got it defending you."

Suddenly, she was speechless.

"Theo said he told you about everything. Says you're scared of it." He grabbed her hands and kissed her fingers one by one, while he stared into her eyes.

Miranda shivered. Her body responded to him so fast her knees went weak. She cleared her throat and backed up a pace, needing to put some distance between them. "I have the rest of the afternoon off, and I'm willing to talk." She owed him that much, considering their spirits were compatible or whatever.

"Okay. Where do you want to go?"

She paused. "Don't think this is some kind of come-on, but I'd like to just go to my apartment. I don't want to be around people today." She lowered her voice. "I don't want to risk seeing any more of those things. I've had enough of them for a while."

He nodded. "Let's go settle my bill and get out of here." He started past her.

She held up her hand to stop him in his tracks. "Really. It's not a come-on. Understand?"

"I'll be a perfect gentleman."

She watched the feral way he walked away and wondered if he knew the meaning of the word *gentleman*.

They'd taken Miranda's car to the hospital and then to her apartment. Marco said he'd catch a cab back to his SUV. Soon Miranda was sliding her key into the lock on her apartment door and suddenly the whole process seemed a lot more sexual than she'd ever noticed before. She cleared her throat nervously and opened the door.

Once inside, she threw her purse on the kitchen counter. "Want something to drink? A soda or a beer?"

"Sure. A beer would be great." He wandered into the living room, inspecting her comfy, homey décor. She liked the colors surrounding her to be soothing and her furniture comfortable rather than trendy or classy. She followed after him and watched him sling his long black coat over a chair and sit down on her overstuffed blue couch.

She got two imported beers from her fridge, popped the tops and walked into the living room.

Damn. Why did he look so good there? Why did the sight of him, the scent of him, in her living area please her so much? It really was like she'd known him forever. Like he and Theo were long-lost lovers, men she'd had passionate affairs with sometime in the distant past and a part of her was just thrilled they were back.

It was—like everything else that had happened in the last week and a half—bizarre.

"What's wrong?" he asked her.

She blinked, realizing she'd been staring. "Nothing." Miranda handed him his beer and sat down in a nearby chair. She took a sip from her own bottle and considered him. "Why is that goblin married to a human woman?"

Marco smiled ruefully. "The goblins find humans . . . amusing. They want to exterminate the Tylwyth Teg, but they just play with humans. It's not uncommon to find them intermarrying." He shrugged. "They live among humans, act human for the most part. Not all of them are bad, but the race in general is naturally violent and aggressive. Watch TV much?"

"Almost never."

"Turn it on sometime. You'll be shocked to discover how many goblins hold key places in government and business."

Miranda shivered. Goblins moving themselves into positions of power, like chess pieces. "And if the goblins decide they want to do more than just *play* with humanity?"

Marco smiled. "Well, that's partly why we're here. We hold lots of those positions too. But we have no natural tendencies toward violence, and no agenda regarding the human race. We just want to be left alone, left to live our lives."

"This is all so . . ."

"Mind-blowing?"

She exhaled sharply. "Yes." She paused. "So, Theo told me some interesting things," she said as an opening. "Strange things, like you, me and Theo are bonded together in some mystical way."

"Theo told me some things too. He said you weren't sure

TEMPTED BY TWO    151

about the whole thing." His voice was tight, but luckily he knew better than to mention her sleeping with Theo. That was wise of him. Passing judgment on her for sleeping with Theo before she'd known about the bond she apparently shared with Marco would have really made her mad.

"Can you blame me?" she answered with a smile that she knew didn't reach her eyes. "Two weeks ago I was dating whomever I wanted. I was free. Now it turns out I have a spirit-level bond with not only one but two men . . . two men who aren't even *men*, not even human." She sighed. "It'll take me a little time to become accustomed to the idea."

Marco considered her for a moment. He licked his lips and rubbed his palm over his stubbled chin. "Theo told me you have a friend in a similar relationship."

"Yes."

"Is she happy?"

Miranda didn't say anything for a moment, then she stood and walked toward the kitchen. "Olivia is the happiest I've ever seen her. She's in love with Will and Mason, and they love her." She shrugged, staring past the small bar with stools that divided the kitchen and living room. "It's beautiful. Not traditional at all, but still beautiful. It works for them."

She felt Marco come up to stand behind her. He put his hand on her shoulder and she closed her eyes. It felt good when he touched her, just like when Theo touched her. It felt *right*.

"Then what is it?" he asked. "Do you have a problem with the idea of being with two men at the same time sexually?"

She'd joked about it with Olivia, had said Olivia was lucky. That had been forever ago. So much had happened since then.

She shook her head. "A little. I mean, it's a little intimidating. But, it's not totally that." It wasn't really that she was frightened of being with two men at the same time. Physically, the idea was very intriguing, exciting. The rest of it was simply perplexing. The relationship would be double the work, really, double the commitment. She'd be tying her life to not only one man but two.

She squeezed her eyes shut, remembering her mother. Her mother had adored her father at first, had met him and fallen deeply in love. She'd thought it would last forever, that nothing would ever part them. Her mother had never dreamed her marriage would end up the way it had.

Yet, not long into their relationship, her father had become very controlling and suspicious. By the time Miranda was born, her father had starting hitting her mother for imagined affairs and slight infractions—for burning his toast, not ironing his shirt correctly.

Life had been so hard back then. Her mother would leave and drag Miranda with her, only to have her husband sweet-talk her into coming back home. Eventually, he eroded so much of her mother's sense of self-worth, had so effectively brainwashed her, that her mother had begun thinking she couldn't leave him. That she had no options at all and that she was dependant on him for everything.

Growing up, Miranda had walked on eggshells in her house. Her father had never turned his wrath on her directly, but things she did sometimes inadvertently got her mother in trouble. Her home had never been a home; it had been a war zone. Life had become a series of strategies meant to keep her and her mother safe from his anger. It had been no way to live, definitely no way for a girl to come of age. Miranda had grown up hard and fast, feeling as if she mothered her mother instead of the other way around.

Then, when she'd been seventeen, her father had almost killed her mother. That had been when she'd finally convinced her mother to give fleeing one last try. They'd left the house in the middle of the night, bringing nothing with them but a large sum of cash. They'd traveled across the country, leaving no paper trail, and settled in a new city, started a new life. Her mother had been happy for a while.

But none of it had mattered in the end.

Because the man her mother had loved with all her heart when she'd been young—her supposed soul mate—had tracked her down somehow and murdered her.

Marco exhaled, jerking her from her thoughts. "Just give me a chance. Please. The thought of not being with you is like being denied air to breathe. I know it's frightening, but I care about you, Miranda. Theo cares about you. We would never do anything to hurt you, so if you say leave you alone, we will." He paused. "But please don't ask us to do that," he finished in a heartfelt whisper.

She turned to face him. Miranda was a counselor. She knew better than to nurse such fears about Marco and Theo. For every man like her father, there were lots of good, loving men. Marco and Theo were good and loving. She felt that in her heart.

*Your mother felt the same about your father once upon a time.*

Miranda closed her eyes for a moment. God, all she'd wanted was stability.

She sighed. "Marco, this is all so . . . so not normal," she said apologetically.

Marco drew her close and kissed her. It was a sweet kiss, one she wouldn't have expected from a man like him. This was tender, like he was being careful with her . . . or perhaps savoring her. His lips brushed hers softly, and she could feel his hot breath against her mouth.

She grabbed his shoulders as he pressed his mouth down on hers. She parted her lips willingly for him and moaned when his tongue sought and found her tongue. He tasted her, savored her, nipping at her lower lip, and made easy love to her mouth. The way the man kissed made her knees turn to butter.

Marco slowly ended the kiss and rested his forehead against hers. He was breathing heavy and so was she. "Sometimes not normal is very, very good, Miranda." He sighed, pulled away from her, took his coat from the back of the chair and walked toward the door.

She hesitated a moment and then walked toward him. "Wait. Please, stay."

He turned toward her with questions in his eyes.

"I want to get to know you better," she explained. "Stay for dinner."

He only stood there. "Are you sure?"

"Please?"

"All right." He put his coat back down.


MARCO COULDN'T EVEN TASTE THE CHICKEN he'd just put in his mouth. Every fiber of his body seemed overwhelmed by the woman sitting next to him. She didn't realize the danger she was in, how bad his control was slipping. He wanted her. Hell, he *needed* her like he needed water or food.

The thought that it had been Theo who'd first touched her breasts, licked her skin and found refuge in her soft body made him tremble with anger. He wanted nothing more than to make love to this woman, hear her sigh in his ear, feel her shatter in the sweet, powerful orgasm he'd unleashed upon her.

It had been so hard to separate himself from her, pick up his coat and move toward the door. Touching her was like heaven. Separation was hell. But Marco needed to be sure that Miranda wanted his company. He'd rather reside in hell than push her too hard.

He knew Miranda needed him too. She needed both him and Theo, but she hadn't been waiting as long, and her need wasn't as pronounced as his. She probably wasn't holding on to the very last shred of her control like he was. Marco could only think of how Theo had touched her, kissed her, and had the ecstasy of sliding his cock inside her and joining with her completely.

Marco shuddered. God, he was jealous.

He reached down and rubbed his hard cock under the table with one hand and gripped his fork with the other. He felt guilty about that since she was telling him about her childhood, spilling her secrets into his lap. Intimate things, things that made him want to take her into his arms and kiss away the hurt of her past. Things that made him want to hold on to her and step with her into the future, create a snug and protective cocoon around her. Marco knew already that Theo wanted the same thing for her.

Her eyes glistened with tears and Marco couldn't take it anymore. He put down his fork, pushed away from the table and took her hand. She came willingly with him to the couch and tucked herself against him.

"God, I feel like I've known you forever," she said as she nestled her head against his chest. A whiff of her tantalizing perfume wafted up and teased him. He closed his eyes and stifled a groan.

*Hell.* He was in hell.

"It's our bond, the link we share. I feel the same about you." *And so much more.*

She sighed and his mind instantly made it sexual. He heard her sighing while she lay beneath him on the bed, as he slid his cock into her eager little aroused slit. Marco shook his head, trying to clear the image. All he wanted was to press her down onto the couch, peel off her clothes and bury himself inside her.

Yeah, this was like ice-skating through hell. All his resolve to be a gentleman was melting fast.

"What about you," she murmured. "I feel like I know you, but I don't."

It took a moment for her question to register. His mind was clouded by the scent of her hair and skin, and the feel of her body cupped so intimately against his. "Me?"

She laughed softly. "Yes."

"Uh . . . well, I came from Italy, but that was so long ago I barely remember it. I came to America when I was young, only a hundred and two. That was the year"— he searched his memory— "1806. I was Gaelan from birth. I assumed my father's role. I never went through what you're going through because it was a matter of course that I would grow up and become what I am."

"You say all that so matter-of-factly. But you can't know how weird it sounds to me."

He shrugged. "Reality has many different layers."

She looked up at him and raised a brow. "And women?"

"I've had my fair share."

"Any serious relationships?"

"One, a long time ago. She was another Tylwyth Teg, and a Gaelan to boot. But they found their third and she lost interest in me. There was another, too. A human. I lost her to sickness."

She sat up and cupped his cheek against her palm. "Poor baby."

He grabbed her fingers and kissed them. "Trust me, neither of them could hold a candle to you," he replied sincerely, his voice husky and deep-sounding to his own ears. He licked the pad of one of her fingers and heard her breath hitch. Encouraged, he slid her finger between his lips and laved his tongue over it. He sucked it to the second knuckle, then to the base.

Miranda's eyes grew dark as her pupils dilated. Her jaw went a little slack as she watched him take each one of her fingers in turn and slide them into the recesses of his mouth while he held her gaze steadily, putting into his eyes everything he felt for her and everything he wanted to do to her.

Miranda licked her lips, taking her hand from his mouth. She leaned forward and pressed her mouth to his. It was like a firing pistol going off in Marco's body. He twined his arms around her, his hand sliding under her hair to the nape of her neck. Marco slanted his mouth over hers with a hungry, feral growl.

She whimpered somewhere low in her throat and parted her lips for him. She tasted hot and sweet against his tongue. He wanted her clothes off, wanted her bare flesh under his hands and rubbing against him. He wanted her legs parted, his cock pistoning deep inside her and her little moans and sighs echoing in his ears.

At the moment, that was all he could think about.

"Miranda," he murmured against her lips. "I want you. I need . . . *more* of you." He slanted his mouth across hers again and she aggressively speared her tongue into his mouth with a little sexy-sounding moan.

Marco slid a hand under the hem of her shirt in the back and slid it up her smooth, soft skin to the clasp on her bra. He had it undone with one move of his fingers and her breasts fell free of the cups. Drawing his hand to the front of her, he held one in his hand and brushed the nipple back and forth until it hardened like a little pebble.

Miranda gasped into his open mouth and pulled away from him. She stood and took a couple of staggering steps away from him, like she couldn't see straight.

"Miranda?" he asked, rising. "Are you all right?"

MIRANDA STOOD ON LEGS THAT COULD barely hold her. She felt wet and achy between her thighs, and her whole body hummed with awareness of Marco. "I'm . . . fine," she answered, still making her way toward the hallway. She really didn't have any idea where she thought she was headed.

Three days ago she'd had the best sex of her life on a first date with a man she barely knew. Now here she was, right on the brink of sleeping with another man. A week ago her life had been mundane, normal.

Nice.

Uncomplicated.

It had taken her years to achieve that.

Miranda closed her eyes and reached out, feeling the wall in front of her. And yet, all she wanted right now was Marco. God, she wanted Theo too. She wanted them both at once, kissing her, petting her . . . fucking her.

What's more, she wanted their love.

She squeezed her eyes shut even tighter. Already, even now, she could feel complex emotions for both these men. It was a deep regard, an intimate caring.

It was the leading edge of love, and if she didn't watch herself she'd tip right over the side. She had to remind herself again why that could be a bad thing.

"I barely know you," she gritted out when she felt Marco's body heat at her back.

"That's not true and you know it."

She did know it. One some very deep level, she'd always known Theo and Marco. Miranda licked her lips and swallowed hard. "You know what I mean." Her voice shook.

He put a hand on each of hers, bracketing her face-first against the wall. His breath felt hot on her shoulder. He brushed her hair away and kissed the sensitive place just under her earlobe. "We have time to get to know each other, Miranda. You can't deny the instinctive feeling you have for me, can you?"

"No," she breathed. It was so foreign, so frightening. "You're very . . . *compelling* to me."

He chuckled softly—a sexy-rough rasping sound that made

her shiver—and kissed her again. "Compelling? Well, that's a good start."

"You could be . . . more than just compelling," she admitted with a sigh. She was losing this battle. Pretty soon she'd be naked and moaning in this man's arms.

His breathing sounded harsh and sweet against her ear. Marco let his hands roam over her waist, and then higher, smoothing up past the bottom hem of her shirt to cup her bared breasts. The feel of his large, warm hands on her, and what she suspected they could do to her, made her breath catch in her throat.

"Do you want me, Miranda? Do you want me to ease your skirt off and take you up against this wall? Because I want to do that," he rasped. "In fact, it's nearly all I can think about right now." He rolled her nipples between his fingers and Miranda felt her cunt grow even warmer. A trickle of cream slid slowly down her inner thigh.

"Yes," she said shakily. "God help me, that's exactly what I want."

"I want to fuck you, Miranda. Long and hard, until we both come. I want to make love to you, slow and easy, and draw pleasure from your body over and over."

Her pussy responded to his words as though he'd been arousing her with his hand. Her clit grew swollen and sensitive. "Yes," she hissed. "God, yes."

He reached down and gathered her skirt in a hand, drawing it upward toward her waist. The slow drag of the material over her flesh made her shiver.

His fingertips grazed her stomach, dipped lower to brush over her mound through her undergarment. He groaned low in his throat. "I can't wait to touch you." Marco slipped his hand down the front of her panties. He rubbed over her clit and slid his middle finger into her heat.

Miranda grasped the edge of the window with one hand and splayed the other out flat against the wall. A hard, fast breath hissed out between her lips as Marco gently fucked her. He thrust his finger in and out very slowly, over and over and over. He drew her moisture out as she soaked his hand in her desire. Her pussy was sensitive, hot and slippery with her cream.

He pushed her panties down to her knees and eased a finger of his other hand over her anus, awakening all the little nerves there, then carefully pressed into her. Miranda gasped, then groaned. She wanted to tell him to stop . . . she really *should* tell him to stop, but the invasion was like nothing she'd ever felt before. Soon he was fucking her in both places, in a delicious rhythmic penetration that wiped all thought from her mind and brought her close to a climax.

"W-what are you doing to me?" she gasped.

"Ah, baby," Marco whispered as he fucked her slow and easy in both places at the same time. "Is this your first time?"

"Y-yes," she whispered.

He kept up the easy double penetration, pressing her body against the wall with every inward thrust. He groaned when her cunt muscles rippled around his fingers. She was teetering on the razor's edge of a powerful climax. "You've been neglected in your sex life, but you have a lot to look forward to. Do you like what I'm doing to you right now?"

"Yes," she gasped. She couldn't help but bend her head down a little, offering her rear to him. The feeling of having both her cunt and her anus stimulated at the same time was incredible. The sensations seemed to blend together until she couldn't separate them. She could feel how wet she was, and for the life of her—as much as she should've been shocked—nothing in the world could have forced her to tell Marco to stop.

"Is this going to make you come?"

"God, yes," she panted. "Don't stop. Please don't stop."

"Oh, honey, I won't. I love to see you like this, with your skirt up around your waist and your panties down around your ankles, up against the wall and moaning for me. I hope to see you like this very often in the future."

Those words sent her spiraling right off the edge. He kept up the slow, easy glide of his fingers in and out of her body as she came hard. She felt herself soak his hand as she cried out. Her muscles pulsed around his fingers, still pistoning in her cunt.

"Turn around," he said roughly.

She turned.

"Damn, that was the prettiest thing I ever saw," he growled. He kissed her hard while the very tail end of her climax still rippled through her body. At the same time, he lifted her and kicked her panties away, leaving her clad from the waist down in only her shoes and her skirt up around her waist.

Her hands went to the waistband of his pants. She fumbled, trying to undo them, and finally freed his cock. It was rigid and ready, wide and long. Just the feel of it in her hand made her even wetter between the thighs.

She hooked one leg around his waist as he guided his cock into her and pushed in. "Marco, yes," she moaned in relief at the feel of him filling and stretching her to the limit. It was like she'd been missing a part of herself she'd forgotten about. It had been that way with Theo too.

Marco closed his eyes, splayed a hand flat against the wall beside her head and exhaled sharply. "God, you feel good."

He opened his eyes and kept his gaze locked with hers as he started to thrust up into her. Her hands sought and found fistfuls of his shirt and she moved her hips downward, matching his thrusts and trying to get him ever deeper within her body.

Marco kept the pace slow, so slow and easy that it sent little shivers of pleasure through her. Her back was up against the wall and every thrust pushed her against it, though it didn't hurt.

Of course she wasn't feeling any pain.

She closed her eyes, breaking their gaze. Her body moved with his, meeting each thrust. It was like a dance they'd danced a million times. His cock fit her perfectly. The head rubbed her sensitive place way deep inside her with every inward thrust and his body rubbed her clit just perfectly.

"Marco," she whispered, staring into his eyes. "I'm coming again." She closed her eyes and felt her muscles clench and release around his length and her cream make the slide of him into her body even easier. She bit her lower lip as the waves of it crashed over her.

When the last spasm had racked her, Marco cupped her bottom in his hands and quickened the pace. He pushed up and in, thrusting faster and harder into the depths of her. At the same time, he let one hand, the same one he'd used before, stray back and play with her anus. This time she didn't jerk in surprise.

"You like it when I touch you here?" he growled into her ear.

"Yes," she moaned. She ought to have been shocked and appalled, but instead she found it very pleasurable.

He slipped a finger into the small, tight opening and thrust it in and out. Miranda's hips bucked forward as another climax flirted hard with her body. She dug her fingers into his upper arms for support.

"One of us will take you here, lovely Miranda," he murmured. "While the other fucks this sweet, tight little cunt of yours."

"Uhn" was all she could say in response. She was lost in a haze of pleasure.

He leaned down and caught her earlobe between his teeth, gently pulling at it. She relaxed. "I think you'd like two men at once. I can just imagine how excited you'd be. Tell me. Would you like that?"

"Y-yes, maybe," she breathed.

He added one more finger to the first and thrust gently in and out. It was just a little . . . *just enough*.

Miranda screamed as her climax hit her full force, this one stronger than the other two. This time her orgasm forced his. Marco thrust deeply within her and she felt his cock jump. He groaned low near her ear as he shot his come into her.

"Ah, hell," he gasped. "You feel so good."

He held on to her tightly after both their climaxes had abated, each of them breathing heavy. Finally, Marco pulled out of her and hugged her to him, kissing over her forehead, face and mouth and tangling his hand through her hair.

"Stay with me tonight," she murmured into the curve of his throat. The words were out of her mouth before she'd even thought to say them.

Marco stilled against her. He tipped her face to his. "Really?"

She licked her lips and glanced away, hardly believing she'd asked him. "I want to sleep beside you tonight and wake up next to you in the morning."

"Theo will be jealous," he said with a note of amusement in his voice.

She smiled, trying hard to ignore the feeling that she actually wanted to be sleeping *between* the two men.

They took a shower together, each soaping the other's body until they were ready for each other again. They collapsed onto the bed, their hair and skin still damp, kissing and exploring each other with eager, busy hands and mouths.

Miranda couldn't believe how beautiful Marco was. He was muscular, but not *too* muscular. His chest was lovely and powerful, but not *too* ripped, like a weight lifter's. His waist tapered narrowly and his ass was the cutest thing she'd ever seen. She couldn't seem to keep her hands off it.

She licked and kissed the excess water off his shoulder as he rolled her beneath him and parted her thighs with his knee. He made her feel drugged with desire, like the whole world could blow up around them and she wouldn't even care. Miranda felt completely immersed in him and she loved it.

Beyond her window came the first pattering of rain and a clap of thunder. It made what she now shared with Marco seem even more cozy and intimate.

She let him settle into the cradle of her pelvis, his cock resting against the entrance of her cunt. They stayed that way for several heartbeats, Marco staring down at her with something like amazement in his eyes. His damp hair shadowed his face, swept across his brow. Outside the rain increased along with the lightning and thunder. It felt comfortable, nice to be in Marco's arms while outside a thunderstorm raged.

Marco took her wrists and pinned them to the mattress above her head, forcing her body to arch into his. Comfortable and nice suddenly became passionate and urgent as she felt her body respond to his sexual dominance. Her breathing hitched and her cunt grew hotter and wetter. He held her that way for a moment, staring into her face, then kissed her. His tongue slid past her lips and he took her mouth possessively while he shifted his hips a little and slid the head of his cock inside her. Miranda gasped, feeling the length and width of it stretching the muscles of her sex as he tunneled further and deeper.

He kept her wrists pinned to the bed and his tongue in her mouth as he took her hard and deep and steady. It didn't take long for her to come. The muscles of her pussy pulsed around his cock as she orgasmed. Marco caught all her cries and moans on his tongue.

Finally he also came, shooting deep into the heart of her.

As they curled up together under the blankets and sheets of Miranda's bed, the storm still rattled the windows of her bedroom. She snuggled into Marco's arms, laid her head against his chest and fell into one of the best sleeps she'd ever had in her life.

MIRANDA WOKE TO THE SCENT OF COFFEE BREWING. Rubbing her eyes, she threw back the covers and found herself nude. Shivering, she grabbed her bathrobe and headed out to the kitchen, where

Marco stood in all his shirtless glory. He wore only his jeans, nothing else, and Miranda had to take a moment to admire the view.

He turned toward her and smiled. "Morning."

"Morning."

He walked to her and dragged her up against his chest for a kiss. Apparently he didn't care very much about morning breath. His stubble scraped her cheek, but she hardly cared. "God, you look gorgeous in the morning," he murmured against her lips before releasing her.

She touched her pillow-styled hair and smiled. "Liar."

"I'm not lying." His eyes darkened. "If I didn't think you were sore, I'd want you again right now."

She felt a sexual flush envelop her hard and fast. Arousal filled her up so quickly it took her breath away. "I won't say I'm not a little sore, but it's a good kind of sore." She bit her bottom lip before smiling and dropping her voice suggestively lower. "If you want me again I think I could—"

His mouth closed over hers, stealing the rest of her sentence along with her breath. Marco walked her back a few steps, until the kitchen counter was behind her. She felt lightheaded—almost faint—from wanting him again. He was some kind of drug she'd had a taste of and now couldn't get enough of.

Marco ripped her bathrobe open and slid his hand within to find her bare waist. She lifted her leg, sliding it up over his hip. The rasp of his jeans against her bare cunt made her shiver and sigh. Just as he slid his hand down to cup her behind, someone knocked on the door—hard.

He stilled, his mouth on hers. Then he swore softly. "It's Theo."

For a moment, Miranda felt guilty. She felt as though she'd been unfaithful. But that was silly. Of course she hadn't been unfaithful at all. She wasn't even with Theo . . . or Marco, not officially. Even if she had been, they were trying to get her into a three-way relationship; therefore she had a perfect right to sleep with either of them.

The realization was jarring and not unpleasant.

She let herself relax. "Do you want to get it?" she asked.

He smiled. "I'd rather ravish you against the kitchen counter, but yes." Marco released her and she did up her bathrobe as he answered the door.

Theo walked in with a tight look on his face. He took in the cozy domestic scene, seeing clearly that Marco had spent the night. In his hand he held a bouquet of daisies. Even though Miranda knew that she'd done nothing wrong, she still felt a pang of unease and could sense the flare of jealousy that emanated from Theo. He obviously was trying to be okay with the fact that Marco had spent the night with her, but he wasn't handling it very well.

She stepped forward and took the flowers. "Thank you. Did you know that daisies are my favorite flower?"

Theo caught her up against him and kissed her lightly on the mouth. "I only suspected, love."

"Want to have breakfast with us?" asked Marco. "I was just going to make omelets."

"Omelets?" Miranda asked in surprise. "I don't think I have enough ingredients for those."

Marco smiled. "You have everything I need," he said, then sobered. There was a notable double meaning to what he'd said.

Both men stood staring at her and Miranda felt the pressure of their regard.

Two men. God, *two of them*. She didn't think she could handle a serious relationship with one man, let alone two, and the way they stared her . . . They both had expectations and those expectations felt very heavy at the moment.

Suddenly nervous, she needed to be anywhere but near them both. "Uh. I'm going to go get dressed. I have to leave for work soon." She rushed off to the bathroom.

# FOUR

IRANDA THRASHED IN HER BED, caught in the grip of a powerful nightmare. Consciousness flickered, making her aware she was dreaming, but she couldn't pull herself away from the powerful memories that assaulted her mind.

*Seven-year-old Miranda heard her father scream something at her mother in the living room. Wincing, she clapped her hands over her ears as something crashed to the floor and her mother's thin, high voice filled the apartment. Miranda bolted off the chair she'd been sitting in surrounded by her dolls. She grabbed Mr. Teddy and crawled under her bed, where it was safe. Clutching Mr. Teddy against her with one arm, she lay on her side and pressed her palms against her ears, trying her best not to hear what went on in the rest of the house.*

*The scene flashed to the small apartment she and her mother had rented when they'd arrived in the city from California. Miranda put clean dishes into the cabinet while her mother sat drinking tea at the kitchen table. A darkness tinged the scene, growing darker. Her mother laughed at something Miranda said . . . and the front door burst open. Standing in the frame was her father, looking angrier than she'd ever seen him.*

*A plate slipped from Miranda's fingers and crashed to the linoleum.*

Miranda sat bolt upright in bed, screaming. The memories that followed the plate crashing to the floor were ones she still couldn't bring into her conscious mind. They were simply too painful. She closed her eyes, willing them away.

Maybe one day she could deal with those images, but not yet . . . maybe never.

Breathing heavily, she flipped the blankets away and stood up. She was alone in her bedroom. The ticktock of the clock on her nightstand was the only sound in her apartment. Part of her was happy she was alone, but another part wished for Marco or Theo to be here to hold her and tell her everything was all right.

Funny how she instantly thought of them for comfort.

Shivering, she grabbed her bathrobe and went into the kitchen for a glass of water.

She'd had counseling, lots of it. All counselors were required to undergo therapy, and she had especially sensitive issues. Miranda knew she did a good job keeping her personal issues separate from her work. If anything, her personal issues made her a better counselor, a better servant to the women who sought her out. That didn't change the fact that Miranda would likely never fully recover from the violent events of her past.

There were some hurts time could never erase.

She took down a glass from the cabinet and went still, staring at the stack of plates. Grief twisted in her stomach.

The phone rang. The shrill sound made Miranda jump about three feet in the air. She set down the glass and picked up the phone. "Hello?"

"Miranda?"

Theo's voice. Relief rushed through her faster than she had time to process her reaction. "Yes."

"Are you all right?" he asked.

She stilled. "It's the middle of the night, Theo. Why are you calling to ask such a strange question?"

Theo drew a breath. "I can feel you, Miranda. Your emotions, I mean. I can feel the ebb and flow of them. Marco is able to do that too, but I'm a little more sensitive in that area. You woke me."

Miranda bit her lower lip, fighting tears. Something in her didn't like that Theo was so connected to her. It scared her. She shivered.

"Miranda?" he asked after a moment when she didn't respond. "Are you there?"

"I-I had a bad dream," she answered in a low, breathy voice, on the verge of crying and trying not to succumb.

"A really bad one, huh, Miranda?"

She could only nod, even though she knew that Theo couldn't see that. The caring and emotion in his voice broke her apart. She might have been able to suppress her feelings about the nightmare if he hadn't called, but he seemed to be drawing all of it out of her.

She hated that too, because it frightened her so much.

"Let me come over, Miranda." He paused. "All I want is to hold you, feel you breathe. That's all. Understand? No demands."

Miranda sighed into the receiver. Her emotions where Theo and Marco were concerned were such a jumbled mess. A part of her wanted to just hang up the phone and not let him into her life the way he seemed to want. Another part knew that in Theo's arms she could find comfort for the night.

The latter part of her won.

She glanced into the kitchen, seeing the stack of plates there. "Uh," she answered shakily. "Can I come over there instead?"

Silence. Then, "Of course. You can come here whenever you like, love," he answered in his low, rich voice. "Do you want me to come get you?"

"No. Thank you. I'll be there in about twenty minutes."

"I can't wait."

Miranda hung up the phone and stared into the kitchen for a long moment, realizing she wanted nothing more than Theo's comfort tonight, wanted his strong arms around her to protect her from the past. She wiped her cheeks and went to get dressed. She couldn't get to Theo's fast enough. Miranda didn't want to examine why.

She dressed quickly and drove to Theo's apartment building in the wealthiest part of the city, where all the bankers, lawyers . . . and Tylwyth Teg Gaelan warriors lived. The doorman of the historic, classy building had been instructed to allow her in. He escorted her to the elevator and punched the floor for Theo's place.

Theo opened the door to allow Miranda in and lost his breath for a moment. Even with a tear-streaked face and tousled hair she was lovely. Perhaps because of her tear-streaked face and sleep-tousled hair. All Theo wanted in that moment was to hold, protect and soothe her.

And he wanted to do it forever.

He wanted to trace every part of her body with his fingers and cherish it all. He wanted to treasure and adore her very spirit, her breath, her dreams and her nightmares. He wanted to love every part of this woman unconditionally. The force of that desire clogged his throat, making him almost choke from it.

But he saw the uncertainty in her eyes when she stepped over the threshold. He saw wariness and fear. It did not bode well for his cause, or Marco's cause.

He led her in and closed the door. Without a word, he pulled her into his arms. Miranda let her purse drop to the floor of the foyer and returned his embrace. He felt her shudder against him, probably crying. She allowed him to gather her into his arms and carry her into his bedroom. He sat her on the edge of his bed and pulled off her coat, then her shoes and the rest of her clothes.

She glanced at the bed, noting the size.

"It's custom made." He explained. "I'm tall, so my bed is long and it's a bit bigger than a king-sized in width." He didn't say he'd recently ordered it, in the hopes of working this out between the three of them.

Miranda seemed to accept his explanation and helped him remove her clothes, murmuring that she wanted to feel his bare skin against hers. Theo was more than happy to grant that wish.

With every creamy bit of skin that was exposed, he only wanted her more, but now was not the time to make demands like that on her. She needed his support and he would give it. Once she was beautifully bare, he tucked her into his bed, slipped off his robe and got in with her.

She molded herself to his body almost the moment he covered them with the blankets, and nestled her head under his chin with a deep sigh. Her hands roved his side, back and his chest curiously and Theo grit his teeth, resisting the urge to do anything but hold her.

No demands, he'd told her, and he'd meant it.

"It was a nightmare about my mom," she whispered.

His arms tightened around her. "I figured as much." He paused, not wishing to push her. "You can tell me about it if you want. If not, that's all right too."

Miranda remained silent for several moments before answering. "It left a fracture in my heart, Theo. I'm damaged. What my father did injured my ability to have relationships. Do you understand?"

"Let Marco and me fill the fracture, Miranda. Let us in and we'll do our best to salve that pain as much as we can." He kissed the top of her head. "You can trust us, you know. With your body, your heart and your mind."

She said nothing in response. She only clung to him as if she were drowning in the middle of the ocean and only he could keep her afloat.

Finally, her breathing deepened to sleep, although Theo couldn't find any rest until the early morning hours. Not with the feel of her body pressed against him and the scent of her hair infusing his senses. He eventually fell asleep with a raging hard-on.

He awoke to the heavenly sensation of Miranda's soft mouth around that hard-on.

A groan of pleasure that started somewhere near his toes ripped from his throat as he woke. He tangled his fingers through her hair as she slipped her lips down his length, sucking him into the recesses of her throat.

"Miranda." He groaned again. "You're going to kill me, woman."

She flicked a playful glance up at him, and then slid her mouth down again. Theo closed his eyes and arched in pleasure. Her tongue danced shyly along the length of his shaft. The interior of her mouth felt warm, silken. The sight of her head at his pelvis and the feel of her hair brushing his thighs was enough to bring him to the brink of coming. His body jerked as he fought it.

He sat up a little and took her by the shoulders. "I want to be inside you when I go, Miranda," he rasped in need. "I want to feel your muscles rippling along my cock as I come."

Miranda gave up her mouth's hold on his cock and let him ease her back onto the mattress. "I have no particular objections to that," she sighed.

In awe, he watched the beautiful woman before him, her blonde curls tangled around her face and over the sheets. She arched her back, stabbing her breasts into the air, and spread her thighs, revealing her pink, glistening sex.

He hovered over her, one hand flat on the mattress beside her head, and let his other hand trace up her inner thigh to her cunt. Her breath hissed out of her as he explored her folds, slicking the pad of his finger through her dampness to stroke her aroused clit.

"Does that feel good?" he asked, watching her face. She'd closed her eyes and bitten her bottom lip. She did that, he was coming to find, when she was really excited. It was an endearing habit.

She nodded.

He ran his finger over her labia, caressing her until she shuddered and he could feel the damp heat of her cunt intensify. "How about that?" he murmured.

"Yes," she moaned.

He leaned down and caught one of her nipples in his mouth as he slid a finger up inside her, widening her, then quickly added another. Her muscles clamped down around his fingers. It was so hot, so tight. He licked her nipple and gently, ever so gently, rasped his teeth across it.

Miranda responded by moaning and digging her heels into the mattress. She moved her hips, helping him drive his fingers in and out of her.

He couldn't take it anymore.

Theo removed his hand from her cunt, forced her thighs apart as wide as they could go and placed the head of his cock to her slick opening. He could feel her heat radiate out, tempting him.

"Please," Miranda whimpered and pushed her hips up against him. The head of his cock slid inside and he closed his eyes from the pleasure of it. He thrust in slowly, feeding her his shaft inch by inch until he was balls-deep inside her.

"Yes, Theo, please," Miranda said. "I want to feel you."

She shifted her hips and he felt all her tight, silken muscles ripple around his length. He drew almost all the way out and thrust back in, making them both gasp. Together, they set up a natural, easy rhythm.

Theo rocked back, watching the thrust and withdrawal of his cock into her soft heat, the shaft glistening wetly with her juices. Watched how the head of his cock tunneled past her labia and speared into her cunt over and over.

Wetting his thumb, he reached down between their bodies and stroked her clit. Miranda thrashed under him at the contact, a needful look on her face.

He held her gaze as he stroked into her faster and faster, feeling his climax rise as hers did as well. Miranda shuddered and then almost screamed as her orgasm ripped through her. The muscles of her cunt milked him as she came long and hard, dragging him to the edge of his own climax, then pushing him over.

Theo sank himself deep into her sweet cunt and felt the unbelievable tremors of pleasure racking his body as he came. When they'd passed, he lowered himself on top of her, wrapped his arms around her and kissed her deeply. He watched her glance around and notice the eyebolts set into the bed's headboard.

"What are those for?" she asked.

He brushed her curls away from her face. "All the better to tie you up with, my dear," he purred into her ear and felt her shiver. He kissed his way across her cheeks to her mouth. "You're feeling better then, I take it?" he asked against her lips.

He felt her smile. "A night spent in your arms cures all ills, I guess. Plus, I couldn't let that luscious erection I felt pressing against me this morning go to waste."

"You're incredible."

"That was incredible. I'm still tingling. I like waking up to that."

"You could wake up to that every morning."

Something dark flashed through her eyes and she glanced away.

Theo ignored it, though it troubled him. He rolled over, taking her with him. She ended up sprawled across his chest. He smoothed the hair back away from her face, hooking it behind her ear. "Are you okay? Really?"

She sobered a little. "I am. I mean, I'm as well as can be expected for a person who watched her mother be murdered by her father."

Theo didn't say anything for a moment, then murmured, "Must be hard for someone with your past. You have not only one man wanting you but two." He paused. "I'd imagine you'd have a hard time trusting any man."

He regretted the observation because she sat up and moved away from him. "Consciously," she replied slowly, "I know you and Marco are nothing like my father. Subconsciously . . . I have fears."

"That's understandable."

She glanced at him. "Is it?"

He smiled. "Of course. Only time spent in the company of myself and Marco would banish those fears." He paused. "It's Saturday," he observed.

A trace of a smile flickered over her mouth. "So it is."

"Would you be willing to grant Marco and me the weekend? Today and tomorrow, here in my apartment. I know it won't be enough to ease all those insidious fears of yours, but it might go a little way toward helping. Plus, it would be fun." He'd been planning to ask her this before, but seeing exactly how afraid she was of commitment to him and Marco, he knew it was more important than ever. They needed to prove to her that they cared about her and they could be trusted.

She grinned. "You're evil to tempt me that way. How can I resist the offer of unbelievable sex with two of the hottest men I've ever seen?" She fell silent for a moment. "Two men I really like a lot . . . on every level."

"There's one catch." He paused. "I want you to agree to be submissive to me and Marco. Trust us . . . just for this one weekend. Let us do whatever we want to you."

She chewed her lip. "Trust . . . today and tomorrow. Two days in sexual thrall to two gorgeous men. Sounds . . . intriguing."

Hope flickered in Theo's chest. "Is that a yes, then?"

"Make me some coffee and I'll mull it over."

"Deal." Theo got up, feeling her gaze on him as he sought his discarded robe. He turned to her. "Are you going to shower?"

She nodded.

"In the hopes that you would say yes to my proposition, I placed something in the shower for you to use. It's fairly self-explanatory." He walked to her and cupped her chin, raising her gaze to his. "Use it, all right? It's for your health and to prepare you for things Marco and I will want to do to your sweet body this weekend."

"Uh, okay," she answered, frowning.

He bent his head, kissed her and then headed for the kitchen.

He and Marco needed to work together to seduce Miranda. He realized that now. It was time they both put their jealousies aside and presented a united front, because Theo sensed if they didn't work together, they both might end up losing her to her past and to her deep-seated fears.

In his living room, he picked up the phone and called Marco.

BRIAN SAT IN HIS SEDAN OUTSIDE THE DARK Gaelan warrior's apartment. He'd recognized him that day at the shelter and had tracked him down, figuring he could lead him to the little bitch who was keeping him away from his Sarah.

He wasn't no servant hobgoblin, working his ass off for a little extra blooded flesh on the side. Wasn't no stinking kingpin goblin either. He was just a workaday goblin, trying to make his way in the human world. His hands gripped the steering wheel until they were white. A workaday goblin who'd done nothing wrong, only fallen in love with a human woman. He loved Sarah so damn much . . . too much, maybe.

It was true that he was so passionate about her that sometimes he lost his temper. It was her fault, though. She always pushed him into it, was always tempting him to hit her. It was as though she liked it.

He couldn't live without his Sarah, and he felt bad about putting her in the hospital those few times. He wished she didn't bait him the way she did, then he wouldn't lose his temper so often. All he needed was to talk to her, tell her that he loved her and apologize. Then she'd come back to him and everything would be like how it was.

Perfect.

But that stupid bitch wouldn't allow him to see Sarah. Then she'd gone and had him arrested. That just couldn't stand. Brian couldn't let her get away with that shit, especially because of what she was.

His lips curled back in a semblance of a smile. She didn't even know.

She thought she was like her two men, the fae Gaelans, the bright and shining Tylwyth Teg. How little she knew about her heritage. He had a hankering to teach her all about it.

But he had to find her first.

Brian's buddies had bailed him out of jail after the bitch had pressed charges. Right after he'd gotten out, he'd tracked down Marco Collins. He knew he'd recognized that bastard from somewhere. Recognition had come right before Marco's fucking fist had connected with his face. Brian gently touched his black eye. He had a score to settle with the Gaelan too.

But not yet.

Marco would lead him to the bitch. He just knew it.

About an hour later, Brian was rewarded for his patience. Marco left his building, wearing the long black leather duster and black boots he seemed to favor, and got into his SUV.

Brian started up his car and followed the Gaelan a ways back, trying his best to stay off the fae's visual and mental radars. He followed him through downtown to the swanky east side.

Marco pulled into the parking lot of a historical building. It looked expensive, classy. Brian watched Marco park and enter the building, while he remained in the parking lot, staring up at the building with a scowl on his face. This couldn't be where she lived, could it? Counselors at women's shelters didn't make that much money. Maybe Marco hadn't led him to her after all.

As Brian stared up at the building, he caught a flash of white at one of the windows. A blonde woman, her arms clasped over her chest in a protective gesture, stared out over the manicured landscape.

It was her.

Brian smiled. He'd found her.

Now he just had to find the right time to take her.

*  *  *

MIRANDA FELT MARCO BEFORE HE even rang the doorbell. Theo let him in and she turned from her place at the window. He wore black from head to toe and a hot expression on his face that seemed all for her. Miranda's stomach did a little flip-flop, watching the two men standing side by side, knowing they both wanted her . . . and cared for her.

God, she was so lucky. Why couldn't she just surrender to this? She closed her eyes for a moment. This weekend she would attempt her best to do just that. She owed it to both of them to try. She owed it to herself.

"Come here, baby," Marco said in his low husky voice.

She walked to him and he kissed her softly. One wouldn't think a bear of a man like Marco could ever be gentle, but he was . . . well, unless he wasn't. Miranda shivered, remembering. Not-so-gentle Marco was awfully nice too.

"Theo tells me you're ours for this weekend. Submissive to us," Marco said, running his fingers through her hair. "You think you're ready for the two of us, then?"

She let out a breath slowly. "I guess we'll see, won't we?"

He smiled in a friendly way, but there was an unmistakable heat in his eyes. "You want us to be gentle with you?"

She remembered what she'd done that morning in the shower to prepare her body for the erotic games that they had planned for her this weekend. It had made her ready for anal sex. Her cunt pulsed at what lay ahead of her, remembering the things Marco said they would do to her. She licked her lips and swallowed hard. "No."

His smile widened and he lifted a brow. "Have you ever been with two men at the same time?"

She tipped her chin at him. "Why? You think I can't handle it?"

Marco laughed and glanced at Theo. "You know, even if we weren't bound by soul and spirit to her, I'd still be head over heels for her."

"I would be too," answered Theo solemnly. "Without a doubt."

Miranda retreated from them, feeling uncomfortable. She sat down on the couch, folding her legs underneath her. "That begs a question. How many women have you been with in your very long lives, and how many of them were you *head over heels* for?"

"Me?" Marco rubbed his chin, considering her question. "Besides you? Two. We talked about this before." He eased his long coat off and laid it over a nearby chair. "I cared for two women before you, but I didn't feel as intensely for either of them as I feel for you, Miranda."

Miranda stilled, watching him, her heart pounding. She didn't want words like that from him. He might feel their . . . *bond*, but she didn't. She was far from ready to hear words like that. "Tell me about the human woman," she said tightly.

"I can do better than that. I can show her to you." Marco lifted his hand and she felt the hair at the nape of her neck rise. The air in the center of the room shimmered and a hazy image of a woman appeared. Miranda gasped and put a hand to her mouth.

Magick.

She stared at the shimmering, flickering image in the center of the room. The woman had long brown hair and was dressed in a long calico dress. The lady smiled and laughed, making her green eyes twinkle in her mirth.

"This image comes from my memories." He paused. "Her name was Emily," Marco finished.

"She was beautiful."

Marco nodded and closed his hand. The image blinked out of existence. "She was the only human I've ever shared my secrets with. We were together for thirty years, until she took ill and died."

There was an unmistakable note of regret and sorrow in his voice. "I'm sorry," she answered sincerely.

Marco shrugged, but his face still wore an expression of painful remembering. "It was a long time ago. I've been in other relationships, but I haven't been with a woman that I wanted to commit to since Emily." He paused and looked at her meaningfully. "Until now."

Ignoring that last comment, she looked at Theo. "What about you?"

Theo came and sat on the leather sofa opposite her. He wore a pair of blue jeans—no underwear, she knew that because she'd watched him dress that morning—a gray T-shirt and no shoes or socks. The man looked good enough to eat no matter what he wore, and especially if he wore nothing at all.

He drew a breath. "There have been three women in my life that were more than casual relationships." He held her gaze. "What I felt for them didn't come close to what I feel for you, Miranda. I'm sorry if that frightens you, but I can do nothing but tell the truth."

Miranda fell silent, considering her words carefully before responding. "You both feel that way about me because of some intangible, metaphysical bond thing between us. You don't really know me. You don't know if you can stand to spend the rest of your lives with me." She blew out a frustrated sigh. "This is . . . crazy."

Theo shook his head. "You don't understand, love."

"Well, then *explain* it to me."

Marco walked into the living room and raised his hand again. The air in the center of the room shimmered in a glowing patterns of different pulsing tendrils of light. It was beautiful. "This is the essential pattern of Theo's spirit, Miranda."

She gaped. "It's . . . lovely."

"We can't access the patterns of just anyone, only those closest to us," Marco explained. The picture changed, the pattern became different but no less gorgeous. It was like looking through a kaleidoscope. "This is mine."

"Okay."

The pattern shifted a little again, the patterns changed and the colors shifted. "This is yours." Marco sucked in a breath. "Theo?"

Theo got up and walked toward it. He glanced at Marco and then at Miranda. "It's fine," he said tightly.

"What's wrong?" Miranda asked.

Theo shook his head. "Nothing's wrong. Come take a look."

Something quivered deep inside her. "That's really mine?" She got up and went closer. It was like a holograph, this magick that Marco used. She had no real reason to believe what he was saying except for the undeniable sense she had that he wasn't lying.

"Do you notice anything interesting in the three patterns?" Theo asked.

She'd noticed it right away. "Yes," she answered warily.

"Your pattern is a synthesis of mine and Marco's, isn't it, love?" Theo said softly. "You see that, don't you?"

"I did notice that, yes," she admitted.

"Here's your pattern overlaid with mine and Theo's," said Marco. "Prepare yourself."

She scowled at him, wondering what he meant, and a flash of white light flared in the center of the room. Miranda fell backward, onto the couch. "Oh, my God!"

"That's what happens when two of us find our third," said Marco. He closed his hand and the light disappeared.

"Do you understand now, Miranda?" Theo asked.

"Not really," she answered shakily.

"Your elemental makeup suits ours, love." Theo paused. "You are the heart of Marco and me. With your introduction, the three of us are whole."

Marco took a couple of steps toward her. "We care about you regardless of this, Miranda. I think I can speak for Theo when I say that we admire you, like you, are drawn to your personality regardless of this connection we share, but the connection makes it all undeniably strong."

"Why don't I feel it?"

"Your human blood," Theo answered quickly. "You're much more human than you are anything else. Give it some time and you'll feel it like we feel it."

She licked her lips. "Let's say—just as a hypothetical—that we all bond and decide to spend the rest of our lives together. Won't I die much earlier than you two?" She frowned. "How does it work for Olivia, Mason and Will?"

"There are ways to bring your other blood to the surface, Miranda. You probably won't have a lot of powers other than a very long life and your seer's vision, but you won't wither and die before our eyes."

She didn't want to ask how. Not right now. She didn't even want to know. Miranda got up, crossed to the window and gazed out of it, over the lawns of the luxury high-rise, over the city.

Near immortality and two gorgeous men.

It sounded too excellent to be true. But would it always be good with them? Would she end up like her mother—happy and in love at first, and then scared and hunted sometime down the road?

Marco came to stand behind her. She could feel the heat of him radiating out and warming her back, could smell a trace of the sexy cologne he normally wore. "You're thinking way too much, Miranda. That's a nasty habit you have."

She gave a short laugh.

"You said you'd give us the weekend. Do you still want to do that?"

She turned around and stared up into his handsome face. "Wouldn't I be an idiot to say no to you, either of you? Of course I'm prepared to stay here for the weekend."

He stared down at her with his dark, hooded eyes. She noted uneasily that she barely topped the man's chest. Knew without a doubt that if he ever wanted to hurt her, she would have nothing to say about it. Marco or Theo could snap her like so much kindling. She shook her head, clearing the thought. They would never hurt her. She sensed that.

"What are you thinking about, Miranda?" he asked in a low voice. "I wish I could read your mind." His eyes seemed full of things he wanted to do to her, sweaty, carnal things, up against the glass behind her.

Miranda licked her lips, feeling her body respond to the sound of his voice and the look in his eyes. "I'm thinking about you and Theo . . . having both of you." She swallowed hard, staring up at him, wondering what he'd do. "Being submissive to both of you."

"Oh, you'll have us both before the weekend is through, baby. No doubt about that. You'll be submissive to us and you'll like it too." He reached out and cupped her cheek in his palm. "I'm glad you're staying," he murmured in his deep velvet voice. She felt it . . . everywhere. She closed her eyes and nuzzled his palm, feeling his calluses and wanting them to rasp over her breasts, expecting him to touch her . . .

He turned and said, "Well, should we go to a movie then? I've been dying to see *The Eliminator.*"

Her eyes opened and she blinked rapidly in surprise. A movie? He wanted to see a movie?

On the couch, Theo shrugged. "Sure, I'm up for a movie. How about you, Miranda?"

"A movie?" she asked stupidly, forcing herself to recover quickly. They were going to start their weekend by seeing a movie? "Uh, okay." She blinked.

"Great," answered Marco. "I haven't seen a movie in a long time."

Miranda wondered if she'd get lucky and there would be necking during the movie or, better yet, *groping*.

They took a few minutes to get ready and then they all piled into Marco's black SUV and went the short distance to the theater. Once inside they bought popcorn and an assortment of candy.

Gaelan warriors, Miranda was quickly discovering, ate a lot.

She noticed uneasily how the other women in the theater noticed her escorts in a very female, predatory fashion. Beautiful women, long-legged, big-breasted women. The kind of women who should be with men like Theo and Marco. The kind of women who looked like they fit with such gorgeous men. She was short, small-breasted and would be called *cute,* rather than beautiful.

Miranda gave them all the evil back-off-bitch eye, but they seemed to not even notice her. Maybe the women thought she was their little sister or their cousin, clearly not hot enough to be with either of them . . . let alone *both* of them.

The nice thing was that Marco and Theo did not seem to notice the attention they garnered. They seemed to have eyes for no woman but her and were extremely solicitous of her, making sure she had everything she wanted at the snack stand, which was a bottled water and a box of chocolate.

Annoyed by the fawning of the females in the lobby, Miranda followed Marco and Theo into the theater. They made sure she sat between them. As the lights went down, Miranda had to admit to feeling quite happy. The warmth of the men on either side of her was comforting. She felt so safe in their presence—even content.

There, alone with them in the dark of the theater, watching the action film flicker on the screen, Miranda understood how maybe—just maybe—she could find happiness with these two men.

THAT EVENING, AFTER DINNER, neither man had yet to touch her. They both looked at her with hungry expressions on their faces, dark looks in their beautiful eyes, but neither had touched her in any way that was unlike a brother's contact.

Miranda was getting frustrated.

They sat in Theo's gorgeous living room, candles flickering on the end tables and on the kitchen counter. A fire had been started in the hearth and it lit the room with a romantic glow. She sat curled up on the couch, talking with them about everything. About their childhoods, about how they'd watched all those time periods pass by. She'd always been interested in history, and seeing it through their eyes was better than any college course she could have taken.

They spoke long into the night. It was fascinating and she felt like she knew them better because of it.

She shifted in the seat. Still, she had to admit that she wanted them, craved their touch. Just being in their presence made her horny. She wondered how they felt.

Were they restraining themselves?

Did they hesitate to touch her because they feared it would scare her away?

Did they think she wasn't ready for them? Didn't want them?

Did they think she was made of glass? That she was so fragile she would shriek and run away if confronted with two dicks at one time? Miranda wanted to show them what she'd do if confronted that way. She wouldn't be running away, she knew that much.

It was time to push a little.

She unbuttoned the top few buttons of her shirt as she listened Marco talk about his father, who'd also been a Gaelan warrior. He'd been expected to assume his father's place and he had, though not without some doubts. Idly, sincerely concentrating on Marco, she reached in and rubbed her skin. Marco stuttered over a word and his gaze centered itself on her hand that was plunged into her shirt.

Theo looked ready to spill his glass of whiskey on the floor.

Yes, they were holding themselves back.

Miranda yawned when there was a pause in the conversation. "I'm tired," she said, stretching. "It's been a wonderful day, but I think I'm almost ready for bed."

They both looked kind of disappointed, she noted with an inward smile.

She rose and walked to the fireplace. As she went, she unbuttoned her shirt and the top button of her skirt. "I guess I need to find some pajamas," she said in a faux coy and demure tone. She favored them with a sultry backward glance. "I didn't bring any with me."

Smiling, and filled with mischievous playfulness, Miranda shrugged off her shirt and let her skirt fall to the floor. Beneath she wore only a black lace demibra, matching black silk panties and her black pumps. She stood with her back to them, one hand on the mantle and one of her knees bent. The fire warmed her bare skin, bathed her in its light.

Everything went silent.

"I think that's an invitation," Theo said finally in a strained voice.

"I guess so," answered Marco.

She turned toward them. "Am I breakable, guys? I did say I didn't want you to be gentle."

"We didn't want to frighten you, love," said Theo. "You've had a lot to digest over the last couple of days. We wanted to take it slow."

She took a few steps toward them. They both looked so needy in the half-light. Feral. They wanted her and Miranda reveled in that power. These two gorgeous men . . . they burned for her. She felt her panties get wet from the very thought.

She took a few more steps toward them and then stopped in the center of the room. Miranda met both their gazes in turn. "I'm not frightened."

# FIVE

IRANDA WATCHED THEO set his glass down and rise. Marco leaned back against the cushions of the couch and simply watched, his dark gaze heated and roving her body. Theo walked to her, around her, but didn't touch her. She could feel the heat of his body radiate out and warm her flesh, could feel the whisper of his breath along her skin. His nearness made her heart beat faster, made her body temperature rise faster than standing near the fire.

Theo cupped her shoulder in one of his huge hands and Miranda shivered. He leaned down and put his mouth close to her ear. "We both want you badly, love. I hope you know what you're getting yourself into."

Miranda shivered.

"You agreed to submissiveness this weekend. You're sweet body is ours to do with as we please." He paused, his breath warm against her throat. "Sure you're ready?"

"Yes," she whispered.

He eased his hands down her arms, moved to her waist and glided slowly up her stomach to her breasts. The drag of his fingers over her body raised gooseflesh, made a whimper of need curl up from the back of her throat.

Marco watched raptly from the couch as Theo cupped her breasts, warming them in his palms. The lace of her front-clasping demibra scraped her rigid nipples with every breath she took, which seemed to be coming faster and harder with every moment he touched her. Theo traced her collarbone with his index finger, and then trailed over the plump of one breast to the clasp.

"Want me to take off her bra, Marco?" he asked in a low voice. His hand rested on the rise of her breast.

"Take everything off her," Marco growled, leaning forward a little.

With a skillful twist of his fingers, he undid it. Her breasts fell free of her bra and Theo eased it over her shoulders and off. From the couch, Marco watched, his dark eyes hooded. His erection strained against his pants.

Miranda knew she'd agreed to submissiveness this weekend, but she also knew exactly how much power she wielded, how much these two men yearned for her.

She stood in only her silk panties and her pumps. The cool air of the room kissed her skin and her breasts felt full, her nipples hard as diamonds. Theo remained motionless behind her, letting Marco drink his fill of her unbound breasts.

Finally, Theo eased a hand up and rubbed one of her nipples, drawing her back against his chest. She sucked in a breath at the welcome contact and closed her eyes against the pleasurable rub of his index finger back and forth over the peak of her breast. Her cunt grew hot and wet.

"Do you like it when I touch you this way?" Theo purred in her ear.

"Yes."

"Your nipples are very hard for me. So lovely. Such a beautiful, responsive body you have, Miranda. Where else would you like me to touch you?"

"Uh."

"You can say it. Tell me, Miranda. Where else do you want my hands?"

"Between my legs," she breathed.

"You want me to touch your cunt, love? Is it excited for me?" She nodded.

He gently cupped her breast in his hand and continued to stroke her nipple with the pad of his thumb. At the same time, he smoothed his hand down her abdomen and slowly, ever so mind-numbingly slowly, past the waistband of her panties to tangle in her pubic hair.

"Spread your legs, love. Shoulder-width apart."

She complied, giving him better access to her aroused pussy.

Miranda watched Marco shift on the couch as he watched Theo's hand cup her mound in her panties, then dip between her thighs. She shivered with pleasure as he stroked her folds and clit.

"You're so wet," Theo murmured in her ear. "So hot and wet." He nipped her earlobe and made her knees go weak. "I think you want us as much as we want you."

Yes. With a force that was damn near crippling.

Marco watched Theo's hand work her between her legs, his gaze becoming more heated, his body becoming visibly tense.

Miranda knew that her panties concealed most of what Theo was doing to her there. Theo slipped one, then two, fingers inside her and began to thrust, and Marco leaned forward on the couch, a hungry expression on his face.

Her cunt muscles rippled around Theo's gently pistoning fingers and she creamed against his hand. She felt him shiver at the feel of her, but it was the only indication that Theo was not in complete and utter control of his lust for her.

Working her breast and her cunt skillfully, Theo had her moaning in no time. Her body felt tense, on edge, and she wanted a cock . . . wanted one of them so bad she found herself grinding down on Theo's fingers. Found herself trying to stop begging for his cock.

Before she could draw another breath, Marco was there kneeling at her feet. He gripped her panties, eased them down and off. Theo removed his hand from her sex and, with a growl, Marco buried his face between her thighs.

Miranda cried out at the abrupt sensation of Marco's long, wide tongue slipping through her folds and lapping her sensitive clit. Theo lowered her to the floor and eased her back against his chest as Marco parted her thighs and pushed her knees up, blatantly exposing her pussy for his lips and tongue. He kept her that way forcefully. If Miranda had wanted to close her legs—which she didn't—she wouldn't have been able to.

And he feasted.

Theo raised her arms. She hooked them behind Theo's head at his guidance. The position arched her body and thrust out her breasts. She felt like she was on display, spread for their satisfaction. Theo slid his hands slowly down to cup her breasts and tease the nipples with skillful fingers. He rolled and stroked and gently pinched them until Miranda was panting.

Theo put his mouth to her ear as he toyed with her nipples and murmured, "Is he doing it right, love? Is Marco licking your cunt well?"

"Uh, huh," she answered, feeling drugged.

Marco had his hands on the insides of her thighs, holding her legs apart, while his tongue explored her labia and licked her clit. The sight of his dark head moving between her spread thighs and the feel of Theo's hard body bracing her from behind was almost more than she could take.

"Damn, you taste good," Marco growled. "Hot and sweet." He eased back onto his heels and stared into her eyes. His blue eyes were heavy-lidded with arousal and she could see his erection pressing against the zipper of his pants. "I want to make you come this way."

She had no real objections to that.

He licked his fingers to wet them and stroked her swollen, sensitive clit. Her hips jerked and she almost closed her knees. "No," Marco said. "Close your legs and I'll tie you up, princess. You saw the eyebolts on Theo's bed. There's rope and I'm not afraid to use it. I want you submissive, baby. Understand? We do whatever we want to you this weekend. Keep your legs spread, or I'll bind you that way."

She licked her lips, feeling excitement coursing through her at his words.

Theo eased his hands down and pulled her thighs apart so she couldn't close them. "Make her scream, Marco."

Marco continued the slow, torturous stroke of his finger

against her clit. She watched his hand between her thighs as he teased her. Her clit had pulled from its hood and his caress of it was so intensely pleasurable that it made her squirm and moan against Theo. "Yes," she murmured. "Right there, like that."

"Is it good?" asked Marco. "Are you going to come for us?"

"Let me," she moaned. She knew Marco was teasing her, making her climax build and grow more and more intense.

"When I decide, baby. I like to see you like this, naked and moaning from the stroke of my hand on your gorgeous cunt."

His blunt words made her shiver. She never would've pegged herself for a woman who was turned on by rough sex talk, but it appeared she was.

He slipped down and caressed her labia, rubbing his fingers through her folds. "Your pussy is so pink and pretty. So eager to be fucked. You want to be fucked, baby?"

"Yes."

He eased a finger into her cunt and she felt her muscles react, pulling at his long, thick digit. Theo spread her thighs a little more, making her totally open to Marco. Marco added a second finger and watched her face intently as he slid them in.

"Oh God," she moaned.

Theo held her fast as Marco pulled them out and pushed back in again. "Mmmm . . . so hot and tight. I can't wait until I get my cock in here." He leaned down and latched his mouth over her clit, while he finger-fucked her harder and faster. His hot tongue skated over her clit and his lips massaged as he found that sweet spot deep inside her and rubbed . . .

"Marco!" she cried as her climax overwhelmed her. "Oh God, yes!" She felt her cunt muscles ripple as she came hard. The pleasure enveloped her body, stealing her breath and even her scream. Marco kept thrusting his fingers in and out of her, kept sucking her clit, riding her through her climax.

As the waves receded, Marco buried his face deep between her thighs and licked her, making sounds of deep, masculine satisfaction. Then he climbed up her body, threaded his fingers through her hair and kissed her roughly.

Heart pounding and breathing heavy in the aftermath of her orgasm, Miranda let Marco pull her away from Theo as he kissed her. She could taste herself on his tongue as it stabbed between her lips in coarse, exciting domination.

They fumbled at each other, Miranda trying to get Marco's clothes off. She pushed him back onto the floor. Behind her, she heard Theo also shedding his clothes.

She ripped Marco's shirt, hearing the buttons pop and fly. Working at his pants, they finally got them down and off and his luscious erection sprang free.

Miranda turned to find Theo behind her. He drew her into his arms, fisting his hand in the hair at the nape of her neck and forcing her head back, exposing the line of her throat. She was on her knees on the floor, between the two of them. Marco ran his hands over her back and ass while she faced Theo.

Theo ran his lips lightly down her throat, trailing his tongue across her skin. When he reached the place where her shoulder met her neck, he bit her. Miranda shuddered at the gesture of possession, the slightest bit of pain. Her cunt grew even warmer and wetter. Theo eased his hands over her ass, delved between her cheeks, touching her everywhere, sometimes bumping into Marco.

Theo released her throat. "I want to watch you suck his cock,

Miranda." With heavy-lidded eyes, he rubbed his thumb over her mouth. "Do it."

Marco pulled her back away from Theo and she pushed him to the floor, straddling him on all fours. He sunk his fingers into her hair as she kissed, licked and nipped her way from his lips, down his chest. She dragged her tongue through the tangle of dark hair at the juncture of his thighs, then up the length of his gorgeous, hard cock.

"Ah, hell," he groaned when she lowered her mouth over him, taking every inch of his cock into her mouth that she possibly could. His hands fisted in her hair. The hardness of his cock against her tongue felt like pure heaven. She groaned in the back of her throat and closed her eyes for a moment, enjoying the taste and feel of him.

She felt someone push her curls to the side and saw that Theo was indeed watching her suck Marco's cock in and out of her mouth. He studied her lips moving over Marco's rigid flesh. The thick, veined shaft glistened with her saliva on every outward mouth stroke. She glanced at him, giving him a heated look, knowing it turned him on.

After a moment, Theo got up, took something from another room and returned. He caressed her ass with his hand and eased her thighs apart. She moaned around Marco's cock when Theo spread her labia with his thumbs and licked her. He speared his tongue into her, fucking her with it, and her hips jerked involuntarily. His hands on her waist kept her steady.

Marco thrust his hips up, spearing his cock into her mouth. She had a man at both ends of her, possessing her, dominating her. Marco's cock down her throat and Theo's tongue deep inside her. She felt drugged with need and passion, yet felt completely at ease with these men. She'd let them do anything to her . . . wanted them to do anything to her.

Theo backed away and she heard the sound of a bottle being opened. Then she felt the press of two of Theo's fingers at her cunt. They were slick with something wet and a little cold. "Spread your thighs for me, love," Theo demanded.

She did so and felt him push inside her. Miranda pounded her closed fist on the floor as she feverishly worked Marco's cock in and out of her mouth. Theo slowly eased his fingers in and out of her.

Then she felt pressure at her anus. She jerked a little, startled, and Theo shushed her. "Relax. You'll like this, Miranda. Marco told me he's already done this to you."

Trust.

Miranda closed her eyes and let Theo have his way with her. She felt pressure in her ass, something being pressed inside her. It felt graduated in size. The object started small and gained in width as he pressed it further within.

She gasped around Marco's cock, feeling pain and pleasure and the burn of her muscles being stretched, all rolled into one. She closed her eyes, letting Theo work it into her ass, letting the pleasure override the pain until the pain only played a sweet counterpoint to the pleasure.

Miranda lost her hold on Marco's cock and moaned. "What is that?"

"It's a plug, love. To ready you to take a cock into your pretty little ass." He pulled it out and she could feel it was ridged. He pushed the well-lubricated plug in again, all the while gently finger-fucking her.

She almost came on his hand.

"Oh, Theo. It's good," she moaned.

"Your body was made for this, love," Theo purred. "You're open for me, taking the plug really well." He pulled it out again and pushed back in, making Miranda moan again.

Marco played with her breasts, which hung over him, fingering her nipples. "Wait until one of us takes that lovely ass of yours with his cock, while the other is in your cunt. Baby, you'll come hard, so damn hard you'll see stars."

She bit her lower lip as the plug hilted within her. She felt so possessed, so filled.

Marco pulled himself out from under her and rested on his knees in front of her. He guided his cock to her mouth as Miranda felt Theo remove his fingers and place his cock to her cunt. Both entered her simultaneously.

Marco gently fisted his hands in her hair and thrust between her lips as Theo eased himself in and out of her slit, bumping the plug in her ass with every inward thrust. It sent foreign, indescribable pleasure coursing through her every time. Her lower body, where Theo fed her his cock, was pleasure blurring into ecstasy. She couldn't separate what was happening to her cunt or her ass. It just all blended together, making her eyes practically roll back in her head from the intensity.

Theo's hips moved rhythmically, his muscles flexing as he thrust in and out of her body, his hands steady on her hips. Her cunt rippled and pulsed around his width and length, stretched deliciously. He rocked her into Marco's cock every time, pushing it down her throat. She had to make a conscious effort to relax her throat muscles so she wouldn't gag.

Marco tipped his head back, his hands buried in her hair, and groaned her name. She could tell he was close to coming, and so was she. Miranda closed her eyes and reveled in the feeling of being totally overcome and overwhelmed by these two men. The whole world had fallen away. All that existed now was Theo, Marco and what they did to her.

Behind her, Theo dipped his hand between her thighs and stroked her clit. "Come for us, Miranda. I want to feel you come around my cock." He stroked her and increased the pace and depth of his thrusts.

Miranda came.

Hard.

She fought to retain her hold on Marco's cock as her cunt convulsed with pleasure and her orgasm crashed over her. Marco sank his shaft deep into her mouth and it jerked twice. He groaned and she tasted him on her tongue, swallowed him down even as her body shuddered under the intense waves of pleasure.

Once her climax had just begun to ease, Marco pulled her forward. She looked up at him, confused, but he only kissed her, his tongue spearing into her mouth. Theo pulled his cock from her and then the plug. She heard the sound of the bottle of lube being opened again.

Confused, she broke her kiss with Marco. "What's—"

"He's taking your sweet ass, baby." He brushed her hair away from her face. "You need to be conditioned to this with two men in your life."

Pleasure skittered up her spine. It seemed incredible that she'd come very hard twice and she still ached for more. The thought of Theo entering her where she'd never had a man before was incredibly exciting to her.

Marco reached down between her spread legs and stroked her clit. "You'll like it," he purred. Miranda closed her eyes as he caressed her. She was sensitive from coming twice, yet under Marco's expert touch she felt the edge of another climax slowly begin to rise.

"You-you just want to see how many times I can come in one night, I think," she said in a breathy voice.

Marco grinned wolfishly. He kissed her as he eased his middle finger up inside her cunt and dragged her lower lip between his teeth. "Mmmm," he growled. "Sounds like a good game to me. I love to see you come, *hear* you come."

Theo pushed her down gently. She ended up across Marco's lap. Marco could still touch her pussy in this position and he rubbed her clit continuously, keeping up a light, perfect pressure on the aroused bundle of nerves. Warm liquid pleasure filled her even as Theo set the head of his cock to her anus.

"Theo," she said, suddenly unsure.

"You're open, love," he answered in a strangled voice. "So open. The plug did its job and you're aroused beyond belief."

She felt the head of his cock breach the tight rim of nerves. It burned, the ring taut around his width, but it eased for him and the burning turned to pleasure. She moaned and clawed the floor, feeling him pin her down with his big body as he slowly and carefully slid inside her.

"Mmm," Theo murmured. "Perfect. So good."

Marco pressed her down on his lap and kept rubbing her clit with his fingers, making pleasure tingle and pulse through her cunt, as Theo worked his cock into her ass inch by inch.

The erotic, forbidden nature of the scenario, the utter and total dominance of having a man enter her this way, wiped all thought from her mind. Miranda bucked as Theo gently, so very gently, began to thrust. Nerves that had never known stimulation flared to life, pulsed and rippled. Her body was soon awash in incredible ecstasy.

Theo groaned. "Oh God, Miranda. I'm not going to last long." He said something in some language she didn't understand, gripped her hips and shafted her slow and easy.

Marco caressed her clit and labia. "Is it good, baby? Do you like that?"

"Yes," she hissed. The feel of having him in her ass was just on the edge of too much. She was going to climax very quickly.

"Come for him. That's what he wants. He wants you to scream for us," Marco said as he slipped his fingers inside her.

Miranda's third orgasm hit her so hard, she really did scream. She screamed and came all over Marco's caressing hand. He stroked her through it, riding it out and prolonging it.

Theo groaned and she felt his cock jump inside her, fill her with his come.

"Oh," Miranda said as Theo pulled out of her. "Oh." She felt both stunned and sated. Happy. Well pleased.

"God, you're pretty," Marco said. He drew her against him. He pushed her hair out of her face. "I think we wore her out, Theo."

"She wore me out," groaned Theo.

Marco lifted her and she snuggled into him. "Bath and bed, baby. There will be more games tomorrow."

They bore her into Theo's shower, which was big enough to fit about five people, washed, and then all snuggled into Theo's huge custom-made bed—Miranda between them. She fell asleep feeling totally safe and protected.

And with a smile of ultimate sexual satisfaction on her lips.

But the games didn't end that night. They were serious about getting her used to sex with two men. Miranda awoke in the middle of the night, draped facedown over Theo's lap.

"What?" she said drowsily. Her cunt felt aroused, her nipples achy. "Oh," she moaned. "What are you doing to me?"

Theo's strong hand caressed her back and shoulders, at the same time holding her down. Marco fingered her cunt between her spread legs, making her cream hard and her clit throb.

"You looked so pretty lying between us, we couldn't resist," answered Theo. "You did sign up to be totally submissive to us this weekend, remember?"

"Mmm," she answered, rubbing her pussy against his caressing hand. She remembered and definitely didn't regret it.

Theo grabbed a pillow and put it under her hips, and then he moved to her head and held her wrists straight out in front of her, pressing them to the mattress so she couldn't get away—not that she wanted to. His hands were like cuffs, holding her down and in place while Marco guided the head of his cock into her cunt and fucked her in long, easy, relentless strokes until the room was filled with her moans and his groans and she came hard enough to raise the roof.

MIRANDA AWOKE THE NEXT MORNING, naked, sprawled across the bed and with two gorgeous, equally naked men stroking their hands over her body.

"Oh, my God," was all she could say at the sight. "Every time I wake up you're doing something to me that should be against the law," she sighed.

"We're enthralling you sexually and making you see the benefits of having two men please you," answered Theo. His fingers grazed her hardened nipples and she felt her cunt pulse. "It's all part of our nefarious plan to have you addicted to us by this evening, before my bed turns back into a pumpkin."

Miranda sighed. "This is so decadent. Really, there must be . . . *oh* . . . rules against this much pleasure," she moaned as Marco delved between her thighs and gently teased her clit.

"Are you sore?" Marco asked.

She bit her lower lip, trying to sort the pain from the pleasure. "Not enough to make me want you to stop."

He grinned. "That's good. Very good." He stroked her labia, drawing her thighs apart. "Ah, perfect," he purred. "Sticky sweet, like hot sugar."

Theo moved between her thighs and stroked her clit. The feel of both their fingers on her at once nearly made her lose her mind. She watched the flex of their biceps and forearms as they explored her. Their heads—one light and one dark—bent together as they examined her pussy.

"It's pretty, pink and swollen," said Theo.

"It's gorgeous." She felt Marco's finger enter her slowly. "Wet and ready, wanting to be fucked again, wouldn't you say, Theo?"

"Mmm hmm." He inserted a finger inside her next to Marco's.

Miranda's back arched and she spread her thighs for them, moaning. The sensation of both their fingers buried deep inside her was nearly more than she could handle.

Theo removed his hand and traced her nipple, leaving a wet mark. Marco stroked her clit. "We've plans for you today, love," said Theo. His pupils were dark with arousal. She glanced at his hard cock.

Suddenly, she wanted to touch them both.

Miranda got up and knelt between them, taking each of their cocks in a hand and stroking them. They both groaned. "Maybe *I* have plans for *you*," she answered.

"Uhn," said Marco as she stroked his thick, wide shaft. "You're the submissive this weekend, baby, although I don't mind what you're doing right now."

She gave him a wicked grin, lowered her head and sucked Marco's cock into her mouth. With her other hand, she stroked Theo's shaft. When Marco's body seemed tense and his groans ricocheted off the walls, she switched, sinking Theo's cock deep into her mouth.

Miranda switched off again and again, wondering who would come in her mouth and who would come in her hand.

Theo got her mouth in the end. Marco groaned and came all over her hand a few moments later.

Satisfied with herself, she rose and stared down at them both. Maybe she could handle two men after all. "I'm hungry," she announced. "What's for breakfast?"


SHE SAT NAKED ON MARCO'S LAP as he fed her pieces of sliced apple. His hands roved her body territorially while she nipped bits of it from where he held it between his teeth. His impressive erection poked into her hip. Once she'd chewed and swallowed the last of the apple, he tangled his fingers through her hair and slanted his mouth over hers with a growl in the back of his throat.

That familiar, slow warmth in her cunt ignited under his hands and lips. It was incredible how much these men excited her and kept her that way. She'd never had any idea her body was capable of this—so many climaxes in such a short amount of time.

God help her, she wanted more.

She whimpered under his sliding, nipping lips and he lifted her onto the edge of table, pushing away the breakfast dishes. Miranda didn't know where Theo had gone. He'd disappeared into the bedroom several minutes ago.

Marco plunged his fingers into her curls on either side of her face and slanted her face up toward his. His eyes were dark, serious and filled with emotion. "Damn, Miranda, I want to eat you up, devour you. Make you mine in every way. Fuck," he swore under his breath. "*I love you.* Understand?"

She found herself touched by his admission, rather than afraid. Marco wasn't a man who spoke eloquently and she could tell it was hard for him to find the words. She reached up and touched his cheek. She couldn't use the word *love,* but . . . "I care very deeply for you too, Marco. You and Theo both." Emotion swelled in her chest as she stared up into his eyes.

They remained that way for a pregnant moment before Marco kissed her again, urgent and tender. His lips slid over hers, nipping and licking until Miranda felt powerless, limp and breathless.

"Put your hands behind you," he commanded. "Flat on the table."

She did it. The position arched her spine.

Holding her gaze with his heavy-lidded eyes, he yanked her hips forward and spread her thighs. Marco stood between them, his erection nudging her clit and brushing her pubic hair. "Better. Don't move, baby. Not a bit." He stepped back and let his gaze rove over her where she sat on the edge of the table with her thighs spread and her breasts prominently displayed.

He licked his lips, stepped forward and threaded his fingers through the hair at her nape. Gently, he forced her head back, exposing the line of her throat, and then let his gaze slide down her body once more. She felt her nipples go hard in the cool air under his slow perusal of her body.

Marco lowered his head to the sensitive spot just under her ear and breathed. The feel of his hot breath and his lips on her skin made goose bumps erupt all over her. He licked and kissed his way down the long, exposed arch of her neck, gently biting her from time to time. Where his mouth touched he left a trail of heat. Her cunt felt heavy in its arousal, thick and damp and swollen, wanting to be penetrated and taken hard and fast. She felt insatiable for both these men.

He nibbled his way over her collarbone, over her breasts and paid such exquisite, special attention to her nipples that Miranda thought she'd come from that alone. She stared down as his sensual lips worked each in turn, causing things to happen to her much further down her body. He continued on, bracing one hand at the small of her back while he kissed his way over her abdomen and dragged his tongue through her pubic hair.

Marco's tongue flicked her clit and she jerked, not out of surprise, but raw enthusiasm. "Don't move," he growled. He groped on the table, found a bear-shaped bottle of honey and knelt between her thighs.

She heard the *snick* of the bottle being opened and felt a thin trail of thick, slightly cold honey drop onto her clit and run between her labia. Miranda gasped and fought not to squirm backward.

Marco made a low sound of approval in the back of his throat and spread the honey over her sex with his index finger, massaging it into the opening of her cunt and over her labia. He worked it into her clit patiently until she was moaning and tipping her head back with her eyes closed.

Then he licked it all away.

Her breath hissed out of her as his hot mouth closed over her pussy and began to work. The man seemed to really enjoy going down on her and—wow—he was good at it. His skillful tongue delved through her labia and teased her clit, pushing her closer and closer to climax.

Miranda's elbows gave and she had to lower herself onto the table. Marco pushed her back a little, placing her feet on the table and spreading her thighs wide. Her head hit a plate and she was pretty sure she had some jelly in her hair, not that she really cared at this point.

Marco slid his hands beneath her ass and cupped her cunt to his mouth, like water to a parched man. He nibbled and licked her into a sexual frenzy. She tried to resist the urge to mash her pussy up against his lips in her excitement. God, he was going to bring her by using his tongue . . . again. He latched on to her clit and concentrated on it.

This morning he seemed to want to take no prisoners. This

was no tease like last night. This was flat-out pussy eating at its best and it pushed her right over the edge.

Miranda shuddered, shivered and orgasmed against his questing tongue. Her soft, passionate cries filled the room, along with Marco's noises of satisfaction.

Once the waves of pleasure had passed and her heartbeat had more or less returned to normal, she looked up to find Theo standing in the hallway, his cock hard as rock. He held it in one strong hand and slowly pumped while he watched them. "Looks like Marco enjoyed his breakfast," he commented, staring at Miranda.

Marco pulled her up and kissed her forehead. "Come, Theo's ready for us."

She frowned. What did they have planned for her now? She took Marco's hand and followed Theo down the hallway toward the bedroom. "Why is it that I seem to never be sated with you two this weekend?" she asked. "I just keep coming and coming and I'm still excited." She paused, considering. "It's like I'm in heat."

Theo turned to her in the hallway and pressed her against the wall. His hand found her pussy and stroked while he kissed her deep and hard, slanting his mouth over hers. When he'd finished and she was panting and weak-kneed again, he murmured, "It's the bond between us you're feeling, Miranda. You yearn to tie yourself to us physically and emotionally. Therefore your libido is running extra hard this weekend, just as ours have been ever since we first laid eyes on you."

"What's the cure?" she breathed against his lips as his fingers gently caressed her between her thighs. Not that she minded the disease.

A wicked smile curved his lips. "Lots and lots of sex."

"Oh."

He grabbed her hand and pulled through the doorway of the bedroom.

"Oh!" she said again, seeing what Theo had been doing while Marco had been busy with her on the dining room table. "Is that for me?"

"Oh, yeah," said Marco, muscling her toward the contraption set up at the end of Theo's bed.

He helped her onto a small platform several inches high. Above her head swung ropes with soft-lined cuffs. Miranda understood the concept. The platform made her tall enough to match them in height more or less—cunt to cocks.

Theo stared into her eyes as he gathered her wrists and pulled them up, securing them in the lambskin-lined cuffs. The locks closed with a *snick* and she was stretched upward, bound and helpless to them.

"How do you feel?" Theo purred as he kissed her face, his hands rubbing over her back.

She grasped the ropes and let them take her weight. The ropes were strong enough that she could probably swing from them if she wanted. "Exposed," she breathed.

"Yes." He eased a hand to her cunt, spreading her thighs, and stroked her with sureness and experience.

"Helpless . . . uhn," she murmured, feeling herself cream against the slow drag of his fingers over her sex.

"Mmm, you like that a little bit, don't you, love?"

She felt drugged. Something had happened when they'd bound her, she'd relaxed and gone limp. She'd given up to them, everything up to them. Miranda trusted them both enough to do that. She knew somewhere deep within her, past all her fears, that they would never hurt her. "Uhn," she moaned again.

"Do you trust us?" Theo asked as he gently worked her clit between his thumb and forefinger. "You know if you want us to stop you just say the word."

"I trust you," she sighed, knowing it was the truth.

She did trust them.

"I don't think you'll want us to stop, Miranda," Theo finished. He closed his mouth over her breast, still working her clit.

Her head hung back and she let the ropes take her weight. Groaning, she decided she really probably wouldn't.

Behind her, she felt Marco slick lubricant over her anus. She jerked in surprise and he held her hip, holding her in place as he eased fingers into her tight rear opening, relaxing the muscles and widening her. A long groan came from Miranda as he gently thrust in and out, murmuring sweetly to her in a language she didn't understand.

Theo guided the head of his cock to her cunt and wrapped her arms around him, gently taking her weight against him and kissing her mouth as he thrust slowly and surely into her heat even as Marco worked his fingers in and out of her from behind.

It was almost too much.

It was like sensory overload to the point where she could barely find the beginning and the end to what Theo and Marco did to her. It was just all pleasure, intense and overwhelming. It stole her breath, her thought, her ability to reason at all. At this point she was completely at their mercy and she loved it.

She did trust them. Totally and perfectly in this one moment.

She wanted nothing more than to please them, to let them use her body to find their release. The thought excited her.

Theo thrust his hips up, hilting deep inside her. Miranda gasped at the sensation of having him fill her so suddenly. Her cunt muscles pulsed and rippled around his shaft. Theo groaned and nuzzled her throat, holding her against his chest as he gently and slowly fucked her until she was whimpering and moaning his name.

"I love you," he murmured into her ear. He fisted his fingers through her curls and kissed her earlobe. "I love you, Miranda. Do you understand?" His voice was filled with emotion. "I would do anything for you, do anything to have you in my life." Over and over he told her he loved her as his cock glided in and out of her body.

"Oh, Theo," she whispered. She felt tears fill her eyes, emotion for him well in her chest.

Marco braced her back, ran his hands over her. His hands slipped between her body and Theo's to cup her breasts and roll her nipples. All the while Theo eased in and out of her.

"Easy, baby," Marco said as he set the lubed head of his cock to her ass. He pressed up into her, widening her and tunneling deeper within. "Mmmm, relax, okay?"

Miranda clenched her hands on the rope above her head at the erotic onslaught. It was incredible. She'd never felt so dominated and utterly possessed as she did now.

"Okay, baby?" Marco whispered into her other ear. "Are you all right?"

She nodded slightly, her eyes closed, and panted. "Don't stop," she pushed out.

Marco chuckled and pushed within her another inch. "It would be hard to stop now, Miranda. You feel so damn perfect around my cock." Another slow inch, another . . . "Awww, honey," he groaned. "Hell, you feel good."

Finally they were both balls-deep inside her and motionless. There was a little pain from having Marco in her ass, but it was nearly swallowed up by the sensation of pleasure.

*Oh God, could someone die of sexual ecstasy?* she wondered through the fog in her brain.

In tandem, Marco and Theo began to gently thrust. The feeling was indescribable. She couldn't tell where Theo ended and Marco began. It was just rapture, pure and intense. Each of them thrust into her, synchronizing their movements.

Miranda glanced to the side and caught their reflection in Theo's lengthwise mirror. She stood in the center of these two powerfully muscled men, her arms straight above her head and cuffed. Both men held her waist, their powerful legs and buttocks flexing as they both thrust up into her body on either side of her.

Her face was slack with lust and her eyes were dark and hooded under the heavy sexual fog she felt. She watched in the mirror's reflection their pelvises thrust as they took her slow and steadily, watched the expressions on their faces and recognized they felt this ecstasy too.

Their groans and sighs filled the air of the room, growing louder and more intense as they all found completion in each other.

Pleasure tingled through her, growing more and more intense until it exploded. Miranda tipped her head back and sagged in the ropes as she climaxed . . . and climaxed and climaxed. She heard both Theo and Marco groan as they, too, both came.

The orgasm stole parts of her vision, she felt defenseless under the power of it. Her cunt rippled and convulsed around Theo's pistoning cock until he gradually ceased his movements and the two men pulled out from her body.

Theo reached up and undid her cuffs. She let her herself collapse on him and they laid her on the bed, one on each side of her. Miranda drowsed in a twilight zone of satisfaction, mostly unable to move or form words. She felt their hands moving over her flesh and their lips kissing her. She heard them both murmur how much they loved her.

"Fireworks," Miranda murmured and then fell asleep.

"FIREWORKS," MURMURED MARCO as he snuggled in on one side of her.

Miranda drowsily opened her eyes. They'd slept on and off throughout the day, piled like puppies in the middle of Theo's enormous bed. She couldn't get enough of them. Periodically, they'd stroke her body into a frenzy of need and one of them would slide between her thighs and ease that need, while the other caressed her clit, kissed her mouth and petted her breasts.

Theo kissed her brow and stroked his strong hand down her arm. "Do you see how you fit with us, Miranda?" he whispered. "You're a puzzle piece. The one that makes the three of us a picture."

*But what kind of picture?* she wondered, nuzzling Marco's throat.

A strong one, she suspected. A beautiful one. But only time would reveal that.

She felt like she wanted to give them that time. She wanted to see what they would be as a unit, a partnership . . . a family.

Outside, evening fell. It signaled the end of an amazing weekend. She had no clothes at Theo's apartment and she had to get up early for work, but she seemed unable to get out of his bed. She wanted to stay in their arms, receiving their kisses and caresses.

Theo must've seen her glance out the window. "Thinking of leaving us?"

She smiled and kissed Marco's throat. "I want to stay," she answered simply.

# SIX

"Bye, Valerie!" Miranda called as she pushed open the doors of the center and stepped outside into the late afternoon. She stopped and inhaled the fresh air and smiled. God, had she ever been this happy?

For the last two weeks, she'd seen either Theo or Marco almost every night, sometimes both of them together. Sometimes there was just rocking hot sex, other times they took her out to eat, or to an art gallery. Theo had taken her on a midnight cruise down the river once.

Every night she'd gotten to know them each better.

And could say she'd fallen in love with both of them.

Fallen in love with handsome, powerful and sophisticated Theo. What woman wouldn't fall prey to a man with the charms he possessed? He could make her orgasm hard enough to see stars and discuss Goethe with her afterward while he stroked her with his strong hands.

Fallen in love with Marco, who was far more bark than he was bite . . . with her anyway. Really, the man was a teddy bear who liked to cuddle after he'd blown her mind—several times—in bed. He was sensitive, passionate and loyal to a fault.

Fishing her keys out of her purse, she walked toward her car. It was clear she cared for both men, and they cared for her. Her doubts and fears still lingered. In truth, they were so deep-seated she wasn't sure they could ever be completely vanquished. However, she trusted both Marco and Theo, trusted and loved them.

It was time she demonstrated that.

Theo had once broached the subject of all three of them moving in together, as Olivia, Mason and Will had done. Theo said that all three of them could sell their condos and buy a house that would suit them all, maybe somewhere a little ways away from the city on a pretty piece of land with trees.

It would be a huge move for Miranda, a large investment in her love for them and a rejection of her lingering fears. It was a bold move, and an impulsive one, but this was far from a regular relationship, and more and more every day she felt that incredible bond Theo and Marco spoke of.

Tonight she intended to tell both Marco and Theo that she wanted to do it.

She had invited them to dinner at Seventh Heaven, a wonderful restaurant downtown. There, she'd tell them everything she was feeling—how she'd come to love them both and how strange it was that her caring for them seemed so deep and so strong. She'd tell them that, despite her fears, she wanted to bind her life to theirs. Miranda wanted to tell them that intertwining her existence with theirs felt natural, normal and oh, so very right.

Smiling at how she expected her men to react, she opened her car door and sat down behind the wheel.

The sound of creaking leather from the backseat had her freeze in the act of starting her car. She glanced into the rearview mirror and saw the goblin, the abusive husband Brian, leaning toward her.

Miranda gasped and went to open the door to get out, but Brian pressed the muzzle of a gun to her temple.

"No," he snarled. "You will close that door, start this car and drive."

She paused, breathing heavy through her nose and trying not to panic. Miranda pulled the door closed, leaned back in her seat and started the engine. Then reached over and buckled her seat belt. She did it all smoothly and easily. Out of habit. Her mind had gone strangely clear.

"Pull out and head down the street. At the corner take a left."

"Where are we—"

The muzzle pressed so hard against her temple it made her yelp. "No questions. No words from you, understand? I do all the talking."

Miranda guided the car out into the street, glancing from side to side for anyone she might know and could signal for help. Unfortunately, only stranger after stranger met her gaze.

Her hands shaking and her heart thumping wildly in her chest, she rolled past Seventh Heaven . . . and down the street. A sob caught in her throat as she pictured Marco and Theo there waiting for her. They might get a sense of her alarm and stress, but they wouldn't know what happened to her, where she was or how to help her.

Brian caressed the side of her face with the cold muzzle of the gun. "I can't wait to get you alone, honey. Teach you to have proper respect for your betters. I'm gonna beat it into you . . . respect." He motioned with the gun. "Turn left at the next light."

Turning left at the next light would put them on the road that would take them out of the city, out into the country. It was the road to the large lake about ten miles from the city. She glanced around out of the corners of her eyes, hoping someone would notice that she was being held captive, that the man in the backseat of her car was holding a gun on her. However no one in any of the cars around her seemed to see. They were all concentrating on the road, talking amongst themselves or rocking out to their car stereos and in their own little world.

They traveled out of town, the buildings gradually giving way to trees and the two-lane highway eventually becoming one.

"I'm taking you to my friend's cabin out on Capawin Lake. It'll be nice and quiet out there." He paused. "Nobody to hear you scream while I teach you. Tell you what you *really* are."

A shiver ran down Miranda's spine. She realized that if she didn't get the upper hand she wouldn't make it out of this alive. "What I really am?"

The muzzle of the gun smacked her head. Pain lanced through her temple. "I said no words from you!" He made a low growling sound and Miranda watched in the rearview mirror as his green gums pulled away to reveal blackened teeth.

Oh, if Sarah only knew what she'd married.

"You want to know what you are, bitch? You're so eager, can't wait until we get to the cabin." Brian let out a strangled laugh. "Your shining fae boyfriends think you're like them . . . Tylwyth Teg. I knew the truth the first moment I touched you." He paused. "You've got goblin blood, not fae."

Miranda's hands shook so hard on the wheel the car jerked. "That's not true."

The muzzle dug into her temple. "Oh, it's true. Whether or not you believe it, it's true. Goblins never mistake one of their own. If your boyfriends pulled up your spirit pattern, they would have seen it. It's subtle, but noticeable. You probably come by it on your father's side," he finished with cruel snicker.

She went cold, remembering the exchange in Theo's living room when Marco had pulled up the pattern. They'd both been surprised by something, but had masked it, brushed it off. She'd noticed it, but had been far too enamored of the image shimmering before her to pursue it very far.

God. What if it was true?

Her father had been like Brian in many ways. He'd laid claim to her mother like she was his property to do with as he pleased. Was that a goblin trait as well as a trait of an abusive human man?

But how could she have a bond with Marco and Theo if she was part goblin and not part fae?

"Don't worry, honey," Brian said silkily. Every word he spoke dripped with undisguised hatred. "I'm going to teach you what being with a goblin is like. It'll be fun." He laughed. "'Course then I'm going to sink you to the bottom of the lake so you can't stand between me and my Sarah anymore."

Miranda clutched the steering wheel so hard she swore it would break. She needed to get away from him, but that gun muzzle to her temple precluded any of the plans riffling through her mind.

She glanced out at the pastures and four-board fences of the country that zipped past—at the trees and telephone poles. She did a double take. A telephone pole. She could . . . *Oh God*. She could crash the car. She was wearing her seat belt. She'd buckled up purely out of a force of habit.

Brian wasn't belted in at all.

"Once you're out of the picture, I'll find a way in to see my Sarah. I'll convince her to come back with me. If she doesn't . . ." he trailed off. "If she doesn't want to, I'll make sure we spend eternity together."

Cold, metallic fear spread over her tongue as memories rose up in her mind. *I'll make sure we spend eternity together.* He would kill Sarah and then himself. Just like her father killed her mother and then himself. Miranda felt tears clog her throat as the memories she always tried to suppress flooded her mind.

*She'd been standing in the kitchen, putting away the plates, while her mother sat drinking coffee at the kitchen table. A loud crash met their ears and they looked to the door, seeing who stood there. Shocked and horrified, a plate slipped through Miranda's fingers and broke on the linoleum at her feet.*

*"I love you!" her father screamed at her mother. "I love you more than anything! Why can't you understand?"*

*Her mother rose to her feet and backed away from him, toward the windows behind her.*

*Her father raised his hand and Miranda saw he held a gun. "No!" she screamed. But it was too late. Everything was happening so fast.*

*Her mother, face white and eyes wide, looked at Miranda and Miranda saw resignation in her eyes. As though her mother had expected this would happen from the very beginning.*

*"I love you," her father said again softly, and then pulled the trigger.*

*The gunshot was ear-splittingly loud in the small apartment, but Miranda was too shocked and numb to react to the sound. She only watched her mother crumple to the floor, red already beginning to stain her cream-colored house-dress.*

*As if in slow motion, Miranda looked from her mother to her father and saw that he'd placed the muzzle of the gun under his chin.*

*He held her gaze, murmured, "Miranda," with a shiny, crazed look in his eyes, and pulled the trigger for the second time. He also crumpled.*

*It took a few seconds for help to arrive. People from the building rushed in to gawk, some to help. By that time, Miranda was sitting on the ground, cradling her mother's head in her lap.*

*She was already dead. Her open eyes looked glassy, her life cut off way too soon.*

*Right when it had begun again.*

She couldn't let that happen to Sarah.

"No," Miranda said softly.

She spotted the pole on the right side of the road and veered violently toward it. The action took hardly any conscious thought at all on her part.

This was her only option.

"Marco, Theo," she whispered. "I love you."

"No! You stupid bitch!" Brian yelled.

The pole loomed in their vision. Brian cried out and lunged for the wheel, but it was too late. The gun discharged, blowing a hole through the driver's side window.

It all happened in a split second.

The impact brought a terrible, mind-numbing crash and the sound of twisted metal. The impact sent her straight into the steering wheel. The airbag inflated and smacked her with a white-hot blossom of pain that echoed through her entire body. She hit her head against the remaining part of the driver's side window. Incredible, unbelievable pain left her vision black. Hot liquid poured down her face and she knew without a doubt it was her own blood.

Her last thoughts were of Marco and Theo before she knew nothing else.

# SEVEN

HE GRAY JEWELER'S BOX CONTAINING the gorgeous diamond and sapphire ring Theo and Marco had purchased for Miranda sat on the center of the table. Candlelight flickered over the white linen tablecloth, the highly polished silver and the fine china plates. Expensive champagne chilled in an ice bucket at their side.

While they waited for their mate to show up, Marco and Theo drank single malt scotch from short, chunky crystal glasses. Miranda had invited them to dinner tonight under a mysterious pretense, but Marco and Theo had been sensing her moods of late. She'd been growing increasingly fond them, could even come close to saying *love.*

*I love you* were the words they both coveted to hear from her lips.

Marco glanced at the box and opened it, letting the candlelight reflect on the insanely beautiful—and expensive—ring. Miranda had never said she loved them, but both he and Theo knew she did. They both felt those words were forthcoming tonight. They'd bought her a ring as a symbol of their love. It was an engagement ring of sorts, Marco supposed, though their kind had no rituals for such a thing. There was just the natural bonding, a much stronger thing than the human's concept of matrimony.

Abruptly, emotions filled his mind that were so harsh, sudden and bitter that it made parts of his vision go black. Marco dropped the ring box on the table and gripped his glass so hard he thought he'd break it.

Miranda was in distress.

He looked at Theo, who sat still at the table, his face pale. "Come on," he said tersely. They both could sense that it was bad, really bad.

They got up. Marco stuck the ring box in his pocket while Theo left enough money on the table to pay for their drinks and the bottle of champagne, and then they headed out of the restaurant. Once they were on the street, Theo looked up and down, rubbing a hand over his chin the way he did when he was frustrated. "Where?" Theo growled.

That was the problem: they could feel Miranda's tumultuous emotions, but they had no idea where to find her.

Marco's fists clenched. "I don't know."

"Can you remote view?" Theo asked tightly.

Remote viewing was one of Marco's abilities, but it was unreliable and difficult to do. It might bring them a little information, but not much. He closed his eyes and honed in on his mate's feelings, focusing every bit of his power on them.

"I see the interior of a car. It's driving down . . . a country road." The vision went black. That's all he was going to get. "Fuck," he swore violently. "That's all I got."

Miranda's emotions spiked and then . . . nothing.

"What the hell just happened?" asked Theo. "I can't feel her anymore. I can't feel anything coming from her at all."

"Been knocked unconscious, maybe."

"You saw a car? She was driving?"

Marco shook his head. "I don't know if she was driving or not. She could've been a passenger. I don't even know if what I saw has anything to do with Miranda."

"We have to assume it does. Did you recognize anything? Landmarks?"

"It was the country . . . pasture, black four-board fences."

Theo swore under his breath. "Come on, we'll take my car. Fastest way out of town is Capawin Trail. Logic says that in the time it took her to leave work and for us to feel her distress, that's the most likely route."

They got into Theo's silver BMW and headed off as fast as they could in that direction. There still wasn't the slightest flicker of emotion coming from Miranda and that was a bad sign.

Both men were stoic as they raced through the city and down the two-lane country road that led out into the more rural part of the state. They didn't say a word as they passed pasture after pasture.

Marco was more and more sure that this was the direction he'd seen the car going in, but they were flying blind. If whoever had Miranda had rendered her unconscious, Marco had no chance to remote view through her eyes anymore.

Marco was staring out the window, trying to get a fix on Miranda when Theo sucked in a breath next to him. "What the hell is that ahead?"

His head snapped up to see a line of cars backed up and the

flashing lights of fire trucks, police and ambulances. "An accident." He paused as the realization hit him. "Fuck. Do you think that Miranda could have been in that crash?"

A muscle worked in Theo's jaw. It made sense. It would explain the abrupt cessation of Miranda's emotions. "Hold on." He guided the car onto the shoulder to bypass the line of the cars that were backed up as a result of the accident. It was at a standstill and people had parked and were walking around. "We're going to find out."

Dread grew in Marco's stomach as they reached the scene. It was Miranda's blue sedan all right . . . wrapped around an electricity pole. Theo's expression was grim. He found a place to park and they got out of the car, heading toward the wreck. Marco could barely look—hot, twisted metal, broken glass. Power lines had come down from the broken pole and lay like dangerous snakes on the ground around the accident scene.

Where was Miranda?

Both Theo and Marco began to walk toward the car, but a uniformed policeman walked out in front of them, his hand raised. "Stop where you are and go back to your vehicle. Can't you see the downed power lines? Professionals only past this point."

Theo began to raise his hand, to cast a charm over him. Marco slapped his hand down. They were both upset and not thinking straight.

Marco knew how Theo felt. He had to restrain himself from punching the cop out. "We know the person who owns that car," Marco explained through gritted teeth. "A woman. Is she okay?"

He couldn't tear his gaze away from the wreck. It looked like no one could've come out of there alive. Something tightened in his throat and stole his breath. A strange calm had stolen over him. Somewhere in the back of his mind, disbelief reigned. He refused to fully accept the scene in front of him.

The cop jerked his head toward the ambulance that was just pulling away from the scene. "They're taking her to Mercy Medical. Sorry, guys, I don't know her status. I know they worked a long time to get her free of the car."

Marco exhaled in relief. She was alive. That was something, at least.

"Did you know the man who was with her?" the cop asked.

"Man?" Theo asked.

"I'm sorry if you did because he didn't survive. About five eight, two hundred and fifty pounds, brown hair. ID in his wallet said Brian Simpson."

Marco sucked in a breath. All the pieces were starting to fall into place. "No, we didn't know him."

"Well, head on down to Mercy Medical if you want. That's where we took the girl."

Theo thanked the cop, and Marco looked over at a second ambulance where they were loading a body bag. Brian Simpson, the bastard who'd accosted Miranda at the shelter. The goblin who'd married a human woman and regularly used her as a punching bag.

Good riddance.

Bastard had fixated on Miranda for some reason. "Fuck," Marco swore as he got into the car and Theo started to pull away. "I should've seen it coming, should've suspected."

"Marco, don't beat yourself up. You couldn't have known that guy would come after her."

"He was probably pissed that Miranda pressed charges against him."

"Let's just get to the hospital. This isn't over yet."

Theo drove like the wind back into the city and to Mercy Medical.

SHE LOOKED SO PALE AND FRAGILE IN THE BED.

Theo stood nearby and looked down at the woman he loved more than life itself. Tubes and hoses connected her to beeping, humming machines. Her face and body were a mass of bruises and bandages. Her arm and one of her legs were broken, plus several of her ribs.

Worse, she hadn't woken up.

The doctors said she'd been badly traumatized in the accident and might *never* wake up.

He wanted to get into the bed with her, pull her close to him so he could feel the beat of her heart, her body's warmth and the gentle rise and fall of her chest, just to assure himself that she lived.

Marco stood at the end of the bed. Theo knew he still had the ring box in his pocket. Theo also knew that Marco was blaming himself for Miranda's abduction and accident and would probably never forgive himself.

Theo glanced around to make sure that no one could hear what he was about to say. They'd been able to flirt their way into Miranda's room via the nurses at the nursing station. They'd told them that they were Miranda's close friends and her only real family. It hadn't even been a lie. The fact that they'd moved her into a private room and were paying for all her medical bills had swayed the nurses somewhat as well.

"We need to give her our blood," said Theo softly.

"If she never wakes up . . . it's a risk. She could lay in a coma for a very, very long time." He paused. "And we'd be binding her to us without her permission."

"I know. She's part goblin." He paused. "You saw that as clearly as I did. If she were part fae, she would need goblin blood and that would be more complicated. But being part goblin, she needs the pure blood of the fae to bind and activate her goblin DNA. It will make her stronger." He paused. "She might survive this with our blood."

Marco stared down at her for several moments. "I'll be back," he said quietly and slipped from the room with a whisper of his black duster.

Theo stared down at Miranda, wondering what had happened. They were pretty sure that Brian had abducted her. They now knew the cops had found a gun at the scene of the accident. Miranda's policeman friend Craig had told them that.

After that, they had several theories about what might have occurred. According to the paramedics, she'd been driving. Theo and Marco thought either she'd been battling with the goblin and had crashed the car, something happened on the road to cause the accident, or . . . she'd crashed the car on purpose.

He rubbed a hand over his face wearily, feeling a heavy weight in his chest. God, he just wanted her back, whole and safe in his arms. He'd give anything for that. Theo felt helpless and he knew

Marco felt the same way. The goblin had died in the car crash, so there wasn't even any way for them to take vengeance for Miranda.

Of course, if Miranda had crashed the car on purpose, she'd already taken her own vengeance.

A feminine gasp of dismay made Theo turn.

"Mira," Olivia said softly, putting her hand to her mouth and slowly approaching Miranda's bedside. "Oh, no." She shook her head, looking at Theo. "This can't be. It isn't possible."

"I wish we were all just having a nightmare," replied Theo wearily.

Olivia's eyes were filled with tears. "So . . . they don't know if she'll . . . ever wake up?"

Theo said nothing, but he knew the answer lay plainly in his eyes.

Olivia looked back at Miranda and sniffled. "I don't have to ask if you're in love with her," she said softly. "Or Marco. I know the process. Have you bonded her yet?"

A muscle moved in his jaw. "Marco went to find a syringe."

She frowned. "You have a vial of goblin blood with you?"

He paused. "Olivia, there's something you should know."

Olivia looked at him with dread in her eyes. "No more bad news, please."

"It's not bad or good. It's just a fact. A surprising fact." He licked his lips. "Miranda is actually part goblin, not part fae as we assumed."

"Really?" She frowned and looked at her friend. "How odd."

"They're just rare. Rarer than fae and human crossbreeds. I'd make a guess Miranda only has a little blood, passed down somewhere from within her family tree. We saw it clearly, however, when we pulled up her spirit pattern."

Olivia chewed her lower lip. "So you're injecting your blood into her to make the bond."

"Yes, well, I'll blend Marco's blood with mine and inject the mix."

"It should make her stronger. Maybe she'll heal herself."

"That's the gamble we're taking. The thing is . . . she never gave us permission to do this. I-I don't know how she'll feel, linking her life to ours," he finished miserably.

Olivia smiled and walked toward him. She reached up and cupped his cheek in her palm. Her voice was warm when she spoke. "She loves you back, Theo, you and Marco both. Believe me, I'm her best friend. She is a sister to me. I see it all the time when she talks about you or looks at you." She sighed. "Believe me when I say that her caring for you goes every bit as deeply as mine for my men."

The sound of Marco's duster came from the doorway. He walked to them both and opened his palm. In it lay a syringe in a plastic package. He ripped the package open with his teeth and took out the syringe.

Olivia watched as Marco and Theo went to stand at Miranda's bedside. Marco rolled up his sleeve and Theo took some blood from his arm. Then Theo rolled up his sleeve and Marco did the same.

Theo held the syringe up to the light, seeing their blood mixing.

A nurse rolled a cart toward the door and Theo quickly put down the syringe.

Olivia moved fast. "Excuse me," she called to the nurse as she blocked her entrance to the room. "I have a few questions about my friend's condition . . ."

Their voices seemed to fade away. Theo looked at Marco and then injected their blood into Miranda's frail-looking arm.

Marco took the ring box from his pocket and slipped the sapphire and diamond ring onto her thin finger.

Together, they stared down at her.

It was a question of time.

THREE WEEKS.

Marco sat in the hospital chair by Miranda's bed and hung his head. Either he or Theo were here every moment, listening to the gentle hissing and beeping of the machines that surrounded Miranda.

She never woke.

She'd healed, though, much faster than normal. It perplexed the doctors. They told them she'd always been a fast healer, but of course that thin explanation only went so far.

Marco raised his head and ran his hand over his face. He hadn't shaved in a while and stubble pricked his skin. For several moments, he watched the gentle rise and fall of her chest. A nurse came in and asked him if he wanted something. He shook his head. She smiled sadly at him and left him alone.

God, the time just seemed to inch by. Would she never wake up? Would she sleep out her whole, now very long life? Marco shuddered as grief clenched somewhere near his heart. He couldn't live without her. Not now. Not after he'd met her, gotten to know her and fallen in love with her.

He missed the warmth of her body, the sound of her voice, her gentle smile. He missed the way the sun glinted in her curls. He missed her laughter and even her tears.

The universe couldn't be so cruel. It *had* to give her back.

Anger surged through him. Clenching his fists, he looked skyward. There was no one to direct his rage at. The goblin was dead and fate was too vast and intangible to fight.

Marco got up and, for the fiftieth time that day, went to Miranda's bedside. He reached out and smoothed her lank hair away from her pale face. He could trace the fine blue veins under her skin. All her bruises and cuts had healed and faded. Her broken bones had mended. All as a result of infusing her with their blood and activating her goblin DNA. It hadn't healed whatever had happened in her brain, however. It was possible that nothing could mend that.

Sorrow caught in Marco's throat.

Someone moved in the doorway and Marco looked up to see Theo standing there. Theo looked about as bad as Marco felt. He walked over to stand on the other side of Miranda's bed to look down on her.

"No change," said Marco unnecessarily.

Theo nodded and picked up Miranda's small hand in his own. "Come back to us, Miranda," he said. *"Tae onae su tae maelavicti."*

It meant *we need you or we'll die* in the old language.

Marco picked up her other hand and rubbed his thumb across her chilled flesh. *"Tae onae amouraei."* We love you. He lowered his head to her lips and kissed her.

Maybe he thought the words, the kiss and the emotions coursing between himself and Theo might wake her.

He was wrong.

She didn't stir, and after a few moments, he and Theo stepped back away from the bed. They both sat down in chairs and settled in for the long, long night.

At some point, Marco drifted off to sleep and dreamed about the time before Miranda's accident. Of how he and Theo were jealous of each other at first, but now they were one—united in both love and sorrow.

Something woke him and Marco groaned, finding himself in an uncomfortable position in the stiff-backed chair he sat in. The room was dark, save for the glow that spilled in from the hallway. Beside him, in another chair, Theo also slept.

The sound came again, a rustling near Miranda's bed.

Suddenly alert, Marco rose to his feet and inched closer. The rustling sound, like blankets being moved, came again. He reached her bedside and saw the most beautiful thing he'd ever seen—Miranda's wide blue-green eyes open.

"Miranda," he breathed, smiling.

She smiled back at him and took his hand, squeezing with weak fingers. The ring glinted on her finger. She tried to remove the tube from her mouth, but seemed unable to manage it. Marco pulled it gently from her lips.

"Marco," she croaked. It was the most gorgeous sound ever to his ears. Music.

"Theo!" Marco called. "Theo, she's awake."

Theo came awake as if someone had shot a gun in the room. He rushed to her bedside. "Miranda." His voice broke. "We were afraid we'd never see your pretty smile again, love. You've been sleeping on us."

"How long?" she asked.

"Over three weeks," Marco answered.

Her eyes widened. She seemed unable to talk or move very well, undoubtedly a result of being immobile for so long.

Theo sought the nurse's call button and pushed it.

Marco smoothed her hair away from her brow and she closed her eyes and sighed at his touch. "God, I'm so happy you've come back to us," he said with emotion thick in his voice. He felt anger tighten his body. "Did you have to fight that bastard in the car, Miranda? Is that how it crashed?"

She shook her head.

"You crashed it on purpose, didn't you, love?" asked Theo.

She nodded, her eyes filling with tears. "He was going after his wife, Sarah," she rasped softly. A tear rolled down her cheek. "Like . . . my mom." She began sobbing quietly.

The nurse came into the room, saw that Miranda was awake and rushed back out again. In moments she returned with a doctor and a couple of nurses and soon Miranda was swallowed up in them.

Soon, though, she would be all theirs again.

# EIGHT

ON THE OTHER END OF TOWN was another road, this one also leading out into the country. It was this road that Miranda took with Theo and Marco the day she got out of the hospital.

They got into Marco's SUV and drove through the city.

They'd kept her in the hospital for another week, running tests to make sure she'd be okay once she was released. Her healing, of course, had verged on the miraculous because Theo and Marco had bonded her. She glanced down at her ring and smiled, bonded her in more ways than one. In any case, she'd wanted to get out of the hospital quickly before government agents whisked her away to be "studied" or something.

The bright sunlight of the afternoon had nearly blinded her when she'd exited the hospital. Theo had bundled her into the passenger seat of the SUV—belted her in tightly—and handed her a pair of shades. Now she had the window open and was practically hanging her head out of it, enjoying the fresh air. She thought maybe she'd be afraid to get into another car, but no . . . she was enjoying life.

"So, where are we going?" she asked for the hundredth time. They wouldn't tell her.

"It's a surprise," answered Marco. "We're almost there." He turned down a small lane, lined on each side with tall mature trees. They traveled over a small hill and a house came into view.

Miranda frowned, taking in the scene before her. It was a huge log cabin. Gorgeous. With a wraparound porch and gabled windows. The land it sat on was fenced—perfect for a dog—with rough-hewn logs and dotted throughout with trees, bushes and flowering plants. A short distance away stood an outbuilding—a horse stable by the looks of it—that matched the house. It was beautiful, her dream home. It was the kind of home she'd told Theo she'd wanted on their first date.

It couldn't be . . . could it?

Marco parked his SUV in front of the garage door and the three of them got out.

Silence.

The road was far away and the only sound was of the birds and wind in the trees. It was her idea of paradise. "Where are we?" she asked, confused.

Theo walked to her with a set of keys in his hand. He held them out to her. "You're home."

"Home?" Her mind stuttered. "I'm home? What do you mean, you bought this place . . . for me?"

"That's not all," said Marco. "On that key ring is a key to an empty building downtown. We bought it for you so you can start a women's shelter, if that's still what you want to do. You'll have funding. Theo and I will finance you. We've both been able to build up nice amounts of money over the years and we're always looking for good ways to spend it."

She looked from Theo to Marco, speechless. They'd made her dreams come true. "But I," she started. "But—" And then she burst into tears.

Marco and Theo drew her into their arms and she sobbed, feeling stupid. So much had happened. The accident, now this.

The accident had—ironically—healed something inside her. Knowing she'd prevented Sarah from being harmed by Brian had helped her come to terms with her mother's murder. Nothing would ever make it okay, but she felt like she'd at least saved another woman from suffering the same fate.

Sarah would get what her mother never had—a fresh start.

She felt Theo lift her as if she weighed nothing. She curled her arms around his throat and nuzzled the place where his shoulder and neck met, and inhaled the scent of his skin. It comforted her.

Marco opened the front door of her new house and Theo bore her over the threshold. He set her on an overstuffed red velvet couch and the two men sat down on either side of her.

"Don't you like it?" Marco asked.

She wiped her eyes and looked around her. There was a huge creek-stone fireplace, red velvet chairs and couches, strewn with pillows, hardwood floors and matching end tables. The open kitchen was to her left, clearly state-of-the-art. A spiral staircase near the kitchen led to the loft above her with a hallway that led to other rooms.

"I love it. It's gorgeous," she sniffled. She shook her head. "I can't accept this—"

"You must," answered Theo. "It's a gift because we love you."

"We watched you fight for your life in the hospital for over three weeks," Marco cut in. "Buying this house and getting it ready for you was the only thing that kept us going. You *have* to accept it. We hired people to decorate it. If you'd don't like it—"

She put her hand over Marco's mouth. "I was going to say that I can't accept this house unless you both live here with me." She replaced her hand with her mouth. Marco twined his arms around her and dragged her up against his chest with a groan.

"Don't crush her, Marco," said Theo. "She just got out of the hospital."

Marco let her go reluctantly and grinned. "Sorry, couldn't help it."

"I'm fine, you guys. Really. The doctors kept me for far longer than I had to be there, I think." She shrugged. "I feel up to anything you might have in mind, actually," she finished suggestively.

Theo raised an eyebrow. "Really? Well, that's good news."

Actually, she was dying for them to touch her, hold her, kiss her. It had been all she could think of since she'd started to feel better. God, she'd missed them so much. Though they'd visited her every day in the hospital, she still longed for the feel their hard naked bodies against her and their hot breath on her skin.

Being with them both was like being wrapped safe in a cocoon and Miranda had realized that that was the only place she ever wanted to be.

"We were hoping you might say that," Marco said, grinning. "We made sure we ordered extra-large beds."

Miranda laughed. "That shows incredible foresight."

Marco stood. "Well, we've got our priorities in order."

Theo stood as well and held out his hand. "Come on, take the tour."

She rose and took his hand. The three of them toured room after room of the house, which was decorated much the way she'd always dreamed—comfortably, big overstuffed couches and chairs, lots of throw pillows and soft blankets. The colors were blues, greens and creams. They'd gathered her things from her apartment and scattered them throughout the place.

She tried to muster up some anger at their presumption that she would want to live here, but she couldn't manage to command any. After all, the night of her accident she'd actually been on her way to tell them she wanted to take up Theo's offer to do just this—move to the country and in with two men she loved.

The house was beyond her dreams and any expectations she'd ever had. In the time she'd known Theo and Marco, they'd managed to get to know her so well that she didn't think she could've selected and decorated the house any better than they had. Tears clogged her throat again and she stopped in front of a doorway to control herself.

It was that more than anything, more than the house itself, that choked her up and made love swell in her chest for Marco and Theo.

She really was coming home.

Theo guided her into a room.

"We meant this bedroom to be yours. We thought we'd each take one to be our private digs," said Theo. "Though I hope we can work out a way where you spend some nights with me, some with Marco and maybe some on your own, if that's what you want."

The room had a cherry sleigh bed, piled high with pillows, matching furniture dotted the room. A door leading to a private bathroom stood to her left and a patio door with a deck that overlooked a grove of trees was directly in front of her. "It's lovely," she sniffled. "Everything's perfect."

"Miranda, what's wrong?" asked Marco.

She turned and hugged him. "I love you," she said. She looked at Theo. "I love you both so much I think something might break in my chest."

Theo drew her from Marco and pulled her against him. "We know, Miranda."

"But I never said it out loud."

Marco touched her back. "The words are sweet to hear and we hope to hear them often, but we already knew you loved us. You loved us from the first time you met us, you were just too stubborn to admit it to yourself."

She gasped and turned toward him. "Oh, really? That's a pretty arrogant assumption—"

He drew her against him. "Well, I'm an arrogant guy, baby," he murmured right before his mouth came down on hers and stole her words and all her thoughts.

Arousal flared through her body, hot and heavy. It had been so long since she'd had sex, over a month now since her automobile accident. She yanked off Marco's duster. It dropped in a pile at their feet.

Marco raised an eyebrow. "Theo, I think she's asking for something."

She turned to Theo, grabbed his shirtfront and yanked him toward her.

"Miranda—" he started

"*I'm fine,*" she murmured as she started unbuttoning his shirt. "I've had a week of bed rest when I was already completely healed. I'm fine and I'm"—she got the last of his buttons undone—"incredibly horny." She ran her hands over his hard, muscled chest and couldn't stop her groan of pleasure. "I want you both . . . *now.*"

"Well, milady gets what she wants," Theo answered with a grin.

Marco reached over and switched off the light.